THE WOLF TRAIL

When the Mounted Police's best man-hunter disappears after arresting Alphonse La Rue, Sergeant Dan Keane is dispatched to locate the two men. La Rue is an infamous criminal, the leader of the gang responsible for terrorizing the frozen North and stealing several hundred thousand dollars' worth of furs. But Keane is less pleased with his additional order — to arrest La Rue's beautiful but murderous wife, Jehane. Arriving at the gang's last desolate outpost, Keane soon finds it is more than just the treacherous muskeg swamps that hold a strange secret . . .

VICTOR ROUSSEAU

THE WOLF TRAIL

CANCELLED

Complete and Unabridged

LINFORD
Leicester

First published in
the United States of America in 1927

First Linford Edition
published 2020

A catalogue record for this book is available
from the British Library.

ISBN 978–1–4448–4371–2

Published by
F. A. Thorpe (Publishing)
Anstey, Leicestershire

Set by Words & Graphics Ltd.
Anstey, Leicestershire
Printed and bound in Great Britain by
T. J. International Ltd., Padstow, Cornwall

This book is printed on acid-free paper

1

Because he was now well into La Rue's country, even though La Rue's gang was dispersed and the famous outlaw himself prisoner, Sergeant Dan Keane of the Royal Mounted was prudent enough to avoid the smoother surface of the river and broke trail for his dogs over the higher, open ground. The snow was not yet deep enough for smooth going; here and there a few red leaves still clung to boughs of the stunted maples along course of the the river, and there were still shriveled blueberries upon the bushes. But Sergeant Keane thought too much of the importance of his mission to wish to have his name added to the list of those marked 'missing', that long and honorable roll of members of the Royal Mounted, whose fate is the eternal secret of the tundra and the forest.

And this region, twelve days' traveling from the MacKenzie River station, where Keane had requisitioned his dogs and sleigh, was distinctly within the territory of La Rue. The ferocity, cunning and resourcefulness of the leader of the criminal organization that had spread terror through the North was still a legend among the Indians; their hidden cache of plundered fur, estimated to value several hundred thousand dollars, was still undiscovered. And for the sake of Corporal Lafontaine, Dan Keane could afford to take no chances.

He was too expert a man-hunter for that. Divisional headquarters was worried about the non-appearance of Lafontaine with his prisoner. In early summer Lafontaine had got a message through, to the effect that he had trapped Alphonse La Rue at the head of the Little Fish, which runs into the Great Bear north of Lake Ste. Thérèse.

It is a desolate region of marsh and muskeg, known only to the Indians, and probably never yet crossed even by the police on their patrols. But Lafontaine — little Lafontaine, the expert — had cornered La Rue there, arrested him, sent down the news, and — failed to appear.

When September came, and there was still no word of Lafontaine and his prisoner at any of the Mackenzie River stations, Keane had been picked to go up and find out what the trouble was. Lafontaine had mentioned scurvy, and the authorities were worried. Keane did not know Lafontaine, who was from another visional post, but his seven years of service had made him, in the opinion of his superiors, second only to Lafontaine as an expert man-tracker.

And there was a tag to the job that Dan Keane loathed with all his heart. He was under orders to arrest a woman — La Rue's wife.

The nastiest job that could be given a policeman! But it had to be done, even to the bringing of her in in handcuffs, for Jehane La Rue was wanted as badly as her husband for that matter of the murder of Corporal Anderson two years before. Anderson, too, had cornered La Rue, but Jehane had stolen in and knifed him while he slept, and La Rue had gone at large again.

Dan's one consolation was that, with La Rue and Corporal Lafontaine, the four would form a sort of family party on their way south; certainly Jehane La Rue would be adequately chaperoned. Nevertheless, this part of his mission quite spoiled Dan's pleasure in the other part.

From the higher ground on which he was traveling, Dan could see the outlines of Barrier Mountains to the east, and the foothills of the Franklin Range to the west. Between these two ranges, covering a territory approximately two hundred miles by five, lies one of the most desolate districts in the world.

There the drainage from the Great Slave and the Great Bear, both immense bodies of water held in by the mountain ranges, seeps through a ramification of lakes and streams into a vast swam or muskeg that has never been plumbed. It is the bottom of a bowl, thousands of square miles of unfathomable muck that never freezes, save in the coldest weather; dotted with quickmud, and shunned as a death-trap even by the beasts of the tundra.

As Dan watched, he saw the crests of the Franklin disappear. The pale afternoon sun vanished behind the clouds above the horizon. Across the illimitable distance, the bowl toward which Dan had been descending throughout the day, a uniform grayness was extending like a moving wall.

'Dirty weather,' Dan reflected. 'But that will mean plenty of snow, and better traveling.'

He looked about him to take in the locale. He had left the northern limit of forest well behind, but there was plenty of dwarf wood along the course of the river, parallel to which he had been moving, and he selected a camping spot about a quarter of a mile ahead, where a patch of willow brush would at once furnish him with wood and act as a windbreak.

The storm came up with the usual swiftness of that latitude. Before Dan had reached the camping-ground that he had selected, the dogs and he were battling against a furious gale, sweeping down unchecked from the Arctic, and the snowflakes were already being whirled along like leaves before the blasts of autumn.

It was with difficulty that Dan was able to drive the dogs into the face of that wind, and he was heartily glad of the comparative shelter afforded by the willow scrub, a little distance above the river.

He threw their rations of fish to the dogs, and set up the little tent that he had brought with him. He broke ice and drew water from the stream, the snow being still too light to provide an adequate supply, and soon had a fire started with birch-bark and fed with dead willow twigs, and his kettle boiling over it. Bacon, coffee, and sourdough left over from the morning made a meal fit for a king after the exercise of the hard day's march. By the time Dan had eaten, night was rushing over the land, to the accompaniment of a blizzard that threatened to overturn the little tent even in its shelter of the willows.

Dan lit his pipe and looked out through the open flap, preparatory to seeking the seclusion of his sleeping-bag. This was to his liking, to be the only human in the vast solitude, with his dogs snuggling nose to nose outside and the snow pelting down. He was never tired of his own company in the wilds. If only his mission did not embrace the arrest of Jehane La Rue!

But first there was the matter of finding Corporal Lafontaine. Dan wrinkled his brows. He had been more perturbed than he acknowledged to himself about Lafontaine's non-return, for the little corporal was famous throughout the force for 'getting his man' whenever the said man was to be got.

It was known that the little Frenchman had declined a snug billet at Ottawa because he could not give up the appeal of the man-chase.

Dan was conscious of acute anxiety as to what had happened to the little corporal. It was not likely that he had allowed La Rue to get the upper hand of him. Lafontaine was too experienced a man-hunter for any such thing as that. Still, his non-return and his silence had been inexplicable. He had had the whole summer in which to cover the two hundred miles between himself and the Mackenzie.

And then there had been that reference he made to scurvy.

Well, Dan must push on as soon as the storm let up. Within a few days now he would be traveling along the course of the Little Fish, and the mystery would be cleared up.

The storm was growing worse than ever just now. Dan closed the flap of his tent and crawled into his steeping-bag. He was just falling asleep when a sharp yelp from Miska, the leader of his team, awakened him. Next moment all five dogs were giving tongue furiously.

Dan sprang to his feet, shook off the bag, and went to the tent entrance. In spite of the windbreak, the ground was hidden under a considerable depth of snow, which had piled up about the tent, so that it was with difficulty that Dan managed to force his way into the open.

The dogs were on their feet, howling, and their noses pointing down toward the river. Dan listened, but he could hear nothing. He waited tensely, trying to strain his hearing to take in something beyond the howling of the storm and the whip of the willow branches.

The dogs were trained beasts, and not subject to needless alarm. They would not have bayed unless there were some marauder about the camp.

Yet surely nothing was likely to be at

large on such a night as that, unless some prowling wolverine. Probably it was a wolverine, Dan decided, which had followed his trail in the hope of obtaining some of the camp refuse, or of snatching a piece of meat.

Again there came an outburst of excited baying from the animals; and now, as he listened again, Dan fancied that he heard something more than the howling of the gale.

And then he heard it — unmistakably: a faint cry that seemed to come from far out in the darkness, down by the river. Then, once more, nothing but the wind.

The cry of some hurt beast, perhaps?

No, the cry of a human being, lost in the storm. Dan knew he was not mistaken on that point.

Fastening his mackinaw about his neck, Dan pushed his way through the patch of willows and emerged into the open. Here the full fury of the blizzard struck him, making him breathless for the moment, and almost knocking him over. He drew in a chestful of air, and charged, head down, into the storm.

Instantly he had become coated with ice. The dash of the sleet against his face was like whip-tips, and it was only with the utmost difficulty that he could direct his course at all, while in a moment the patch of willows had vanished into the dark behind him, as if it no longer existed.

Fortunately the course lay straight down the slope, and was short enough for Dan to be able to feel his way directly toward it by the lie of the ground; otherwise it would have been sheer madness to have ventured even a hundred yards from his camp in such a storm.

But that madness lay exactly along the line of his duty, and Dan braced his muscles to meet the wind, and fought it as if it had been a human adversary, until he found himself under the shelter of the slope. Here the force of the gale was less violent. Dan struggled along until the branches of the dwarf willows and alders along the river bank whipped his face and body; and now he stopped and listened for the cry again, uncertain as to the direction from which it had come.

He could not hear it. He shouted at the top of his voice, but his own cries seemed to be cut off instantly by the violence of the wind. He drew his service revolver, and fired it, but he could hardly hear the sound of the shots. The wind was blowing directly off the river, and it seemed impossible that the sound could have carried to any one lost along its banks. Still, that had undeniably been a human cry.

And Dan began to beat a course up and down the stream over the ice, zigzagging from shore to shore and selecting the more sheltered nooks, in which it seemed possible that a lost person might have taken refuge.

Yet in spite of his confidence in his own ears, it seemed impossible to Dan that there could be a human being anywhere within a hundred miles of him — anywhere nearer than Corporal Lafontaine and his prisoner at the head of the Little Fish. There was no mission, no trading post anywhere nearer than the Mackenzie, and that was a hundred and fifty miles to the west of him.

Then the idea occurred to Dan that this might be Lafontaine with his prisoner, trying to make his belated way back to civilization.

And with this possibility in mind, Dan pursued his search as methodically as was possible under the circumstances, now along one bank of the stream, and now along the other, but always counting his paces back and forth from the point where he had descended the bank, and shouting at intervals, until he felt himself growing numb from the whipping sleet.

He stopped. Again he began to wonder whether he had been the victim of his imagination; whether it was the cry of some animal that he had heard.

Once more he shouted. And then,

quite clearly, Dan heard the cry again. It came from a point upon the nearer bank of the river and about a hundred paces downstream.

Instantly he began running toward the spot, shouting at the top of his voice while he emptied the last cartridges in his revolver.

Frantically he beat about, shouting and yet finding nothing. Nothing could now have been audible above the wind, which had reached the top notch of its infernal crescendo. Yet — there was a little clump of alders that had escaped Dan's notice. If the lost human being who had cried were not within them —

He plunged into it like a bull, whipping the stunted growth with his numbed arms. Still nothing! But wasn't that a crackling among the branches, just a little further on?

Of a sudden something seemed to detach itself from the night — a fragment of darkness, cut off from the darkness, resolving itself into a moving pillar of ice that bore an odd resemblance to a human form.

It staggered toward him, and with a low cry that was barely audible, dropped at his feet.

Dan raised it. In a moment, to his amazement, he discovered that it was the body of a woman that he was holding in his arms.

2

An Indian woman was the thought that flashed immediately through his mind — lost, as even she might pardonably be in such a storm as that. But, though the darkness was almost impenetrable, Dan quickly realized that this woman was no Indian.

No Indian woman wore a mackinaw beneath furs that had been put together — as Dan could realize at once — by a furrier. Nor did Indian women wear fur caps like the one pressed down over the girl's hair, which was short — something still unknown among Indian women except in the larger settlements.

Whoever this girl was, she was white; apart from all the other evidences, Dan was able to sense that fact by some process of intuition.

And, finally, it was English that the girl was speaking, English with just that trace of an accent that told Dan her native tongue was French.

But when, to his amazement, Dan heard his own name on the girl's lips, he frankly abandoned the problem of her presence there as being, for the time at any rate, insoluble.

She spoke Dan's name before consciousness had come back to her, murmuring incoherent phrases that Dan could not understand. Then, seeming to realize where she was, she tried to free herself.

'Sergeant Kane — I came to tell you — to warn you that — '

The words were barely audible to Dan as he placed his ear against her lips — so close that they brushed his cheek, and he seemed to be reading by their movements.

'You must turn back, or you will lose your life,' Dan heard again. 'There is no way over the swamps to where you wish to go.'

But the intense struggle to speak seemed to have exhausted the little vitality that remained. Suddenly the girl went limp in Dan's arms again, and this time she did not stir. As her cheek touched his, Dan felt that it was not only icy cold, but frozen stiff.

All speculation as to her presence there, her acquaintance with his name and the purpose of his journey disappeared immediately for Dan, in the face of the urgent need of getting the unconscious girl at once to warmth and shelter. Picking her up in his arms, Dan began carrying her through the fringe of alders and up the slope from the river toward his camp.

It was no more than three hundred yards from the river bank to the patch of willows, but Dan had covered three miles with greater ease under other conditions. With the weight of the girl in arms, the gale buffeting him, and the sleet whipping his face, every step was a struggle, while the snow was already so deep that Dan sank halfway to the knee in it at every step.

But the camp — impenetrable as the

darkness was, Dan had thought it would be an easy matter to find it. He miscalculated, in spite of the experience of years. The howling of the wind completely drowned any sound from the dogs, and the girl, a dead weight in his arms, impeded his sense of direction. The slightest angle of divergence, and the camp was lost.

Dan had actually gone beyond it, and was stumbling on into the Barrens when, in a momentary lull of the wind, the sound of a dog's challenge some distance to his left stopped him.

He had missed certain death by the grace of a moment in the force of the hurricane. It seemed inconceivable that he could have blundered so badly. He turned and sought the direction from which the sound had come. Again he had miscalculated, but this time on the right side. That yelp had seemed to come from a hundred and fifty yards' distance, and little more than a score of paces brought Dan up short among the willows, to the accompaniment of the full-throated chorus of the pack.

In another moment Dan could distinguish the outlines of the tent. He got the flap open, and carried the girl inside. He laid her down upon his sleeping-bag and tried to light a candle, but the violence of the wind, blowing even through the canvas, made this impossible. It was straining against the ropes, and threatened the tent every moment to be blown bodily away.

That was a chance that had to be taken. Dan remembered that there was a little wood left, as well as some scraps of birch-bark. In the shelter among the willows where he had made his fire there was still a little glow among the embers, fanned by the winds. A strip of dry bark and a handful of twigs, and this time the gale was his ally. It caught the fresh fuel and quickly kindled a roaring fire.

Dan filled the kettle with snow, waited till it had melted, and filled it up again. Then he went back into the tent. The next half-hour he spent in restoring the circulation in the girl's face, hands and feet. It was no time to stand upon punctilio and, though the skin still felt as icily cold to the touch, Dan knew, when the half-hour had gone — knew from the little moans of pain which escaped the girl's lips — that the blood was beginning to circulate anew through the arteries.

It was an eerie sensation, being in the little tent alone with a girl whose face he could not see. From her voice, when she had whispered those few words of warning to him upon the river bank, Dan had judged that she was educated — at least, no product of the river settlements. What he had been able to glimpse of her figure — though he had seen nothing of her face — had given him the idea that she was young.

But in the complete darkness of the tent Dan could see nothing at all of her, though he had been engaged in reviving her for a half-hour past.

Romance had entered Dan's life little enough, and in his younger days the white bird had displayed herself to him with more or less sullied wings. That had made him avoid women. None in the least approximating to his early ideals had ever come within his ken. And so what might have been a flair for romance had turned in another direction, into the love of the glorious drama of the woods and tundra in the changing seasons, the beauty of the wild, and the thrill of the man-hunt.

Yet, as he tried to restore the girl to consciousness, Dan felt the piquancy of the situation. The kettle was boiling now, and Dan had mixed tea with a little brandy from his tiny stock, and was trying to make her swallow some of the mixture. He replaced the woolen socks and the small moccasins before she revived, and the gloves upon the hands which, firm and capable though they felt, were not rough like those of a trapper's wife. And when the first broken words came again from the girl's lips, Dan knew that his estimate of her had not been a mistaken one.

'Is it you, Alphonse?' she muttered in French. 'Are you safe? No, you can trust me. I shall never fail you so long as — see that there comes no harm to — '

She was struggling up. Dan heard a gasp of dismay come from her lips as she seemed to realize that she was in strange surroundings, and he put his hand gently on her arm.

'But where am I? I cannot see! Ah, the storm was terrible. I was lost. But who is it?'

'Don't be afraid,' said Dan. 'You're quite safe now. I am Sergeant Dan Keane, of the Police.'

She gasped, and dark though it was, Dan seemed to feel the girl's eyes fix upon him. However, she ceased to struggle.

'You — you are Sergeant Keane?' she whispered. 'Then how — how did I get here? Where am I?'

'You're in my tent,' answered Dan. 'I guess you got lost on the trail. I heard you crying out about an hour and a half ago, and I found you on the ice of the river and carried you back here. You were badly frozen but you're getting along all right now.'

'Yes, I remember,' she answered in a whisper. 'I was — looking for — ' She checked herself abruptly. 'What are you going to — ?'

'You mustn't be distressed. There's nothing to be afraid of.'

'I am not afraid for myself. I am afraid for — you!'

But it was clear that her strength was completely exhausted. Her voice failed her. 'You must not try to talk any more now,' Dan interposed. 'We're both safe for the night, at any rate, and you can tell me about it in the morning. There was nobody with you, I suppose?' he added.

'No, there was no one. But you — what are you going to do tonight?'

'Oh, I can rustle up a bed somewhere outside,' Dan answered lightly. 'It's pretty well sheltered among the trees, and I think the storm is letting up a little.'

She tried to utter some sort of protest to that, but she was too obviously weary. In a moment she had relapsed into unconsciousness, and Dan, after listening a moment to her regular breathing, satisfied that she was on the way to recovery, left the tent.

He had spoken lightly enough, but it was no joke attempting to find shelter in that gale, even though it did appear to be slightly diminishing in force. He made a place for himself among the dogs on the lee side of the loaded sleigh, and found himself fairly well-sheltered. The tarpaulin, as well as he was able to stretch it over him, kept out a modicum of the snow. But it was bitterly cold, the little fire had gone out for good now, and the only thing to do was to endure it.

Dan, huddling down, passed one of the worst and coldest nights in his experience. Sometime he dozed, but all the time he was conscious of revolting nerves and flesh nearing the breaking point. It was too cold even to speculate as to the presence of the girl, apparently with neither dogs nor sleigh. Well, he would learn the explanation in the morning.

3

Dawn came at last, just when it seemed as if he could bear the cold no longer. It came in dull, opalescent gray, with no hint of any sun in the overcast sky, but the snow had almost ceased to fall and the gale had blown itself out into a strong wind. There was more than a foot of snow on the ground.

Dan scooped with stiffened fingers in the snow until he had gathered another little store of twigs and dead branches. He made a bare patch among the trees, and, with some more of the birch-bark, managed to kindle a fire and put the kettle on. He had some biscuit left over; that, with bacon and tea, would have to provide the morning's meal.

He had just got the kettle boiling, and was wondering whether he ought to go inside the tent and make sure that the girl was all right, when she came out. He turned at the sound of the tent flap being drawn back, and saw her standing in the entrance.

Dan smothered an exclamation. He had never dreamed that she was a girl like that! In place of the frontier type that he had looked for, he saw — if not the girl of his youthful dreams, who had been a composite character, at least one of the types that had gone to the composition of that ideal being.

Not very tall, but straight as a young fir sapling, she stood there, watching him. A little over twenty, but not much more, with the figure of youth, dark hair, gray eyes that met his own; and yet there was something about the face that showed maturity of experience rather than of years — that was the immediate impression that the girl presented.

She came hobbling toward him, and Dan tried to give her his hand to help her, but she ignored it.

'How are you feeling?' he asked.

'I'm feeling fairly well, except for the frostbite.' Yes, the slight accent was undoubtedly French, but she was speaking English to Dan, probably not supposing that he spoke the one tongue almost as well as the other.

'You saved my life, Sergeant Keane and — '

'It was lucky I happened along,' Dan answered, in a clumsy attempt to obviate her thanks. 'Won't you sit down on the sleigh? The tea's about ready. I haven't any milk. We'll talk afterward. I hope you'll like my bacon.'

Dan helped her to the sleigh. As she approached it, the dogs who had watched her, growling and bristling, subsided. She laid a hand caressingly upon each of the shaggy heads, and the beasts fawned before her. Dan gave her a tin mug of tea, but she would not eat anything.

'You said there was nobody with you,' Dan began, 'but of course you have a sleigh and — somebody — in the neighborhood?'

'I have nobody,' answered the girl.

'But — you can't have been traveling

alone, without even a pack?'

'I say that I have nobody' she repeated peremptorily. 'I came here to warn you. I know who you are, and that you are going to relieve Corporal Lafontaine and take Monsieur La Rue back with you. But you are on the wrong route. There's no way over the muskeg to — where you're going. You'll die in the swamps, you and your dogs.'

'You seem to know a good deal about me and my plans,' said Dan. Instantly something impersonal had sprung into their relationship. Dan had not even a description of Jehane La Rue. And yet — could it be possible that this girl was she?

It was not possible. She could not have been a member of the outlaw gang that had been guilty of almost every known crime against God and man. In the year during which they had been at large, before the rumors filtering down to Divisional Headquarters had resulted in the sending of a patrol into their territory, they had blazed their way through the north to the accompaniment of murder and rapine among the Indians, culminating in the murder of a Hudson's Bay company factor and the seizure of a hundred thousand dollars' worth of fur.

And ever at their head had been Alphonse La Rue — the craftiest, most cunning, and most cruel of any outlaw that ever blazed his trail across the wastes.

No, this girl could not *possibly* be Jehane La Rue. And yet —

'You have come — from somewhere — ' Dan began slowly, 'to warn me that I cannot reach my destination. Who are you that you should take so much trouble for a stranger?'

'Never mind who I am. Suppose I am the wife or daughter of a trapper. Suppose I happen to know, confidentially, that you cannot succeed. Isn't that enough? The Police cannot ask impossibilities of their men. Turn back, and try the northern route, if you must, when the weather is open — '

She was confused, inventing reasons, and Dan felt his heart hardening. The little glimmer of romance that had been lit for him the night before had vanished. Dan had more than once confronted women who had sobbed and clung to him, pleading without avail for their men.

'Perhaps,' he said with deliberate slowness, 'perhaps you can give me news of Corporal Lafontaine?'

'I can tell you nothing. I've said all I had to say. I came to warn you.'

'For which I'm much obliged,' answered Dan grimly. 'But please remember that I am a policeman. It is my duty to do everything in my power to elicit the information I need, and with which I believe you are able to supply me.'

'You mean you're going to hold me as your *prisoner?*' cried the girl, while Miska raised her head and uttered a low growl, as if she sensed the tension in the very air.

'By no means, but naturally, if you are alone, I cannot leave you to go wherever you are going without dogs or supplies. A woman alone in the Northland is under the protection of the Police. It is a part of my duty.'

'Protection!' she looked at Dan, a contemptuous smile beginning to curve her mouth. There was the consciousness of power in that smile of hers; helpless as she might have been the night before, Dan knew that he was not dealing with an inexperienced girl.

'And so your duty requires me to be your traveling companion to the Great Bear — and perhaps show you the way across the muskeg?' the girl demanded.

'There *is* a way, then?' countered Dan; and she flushed and bit her lip. He did not follow up his advantage. 'Why is it necessary to speak of your being a prisoner?' he continued. 'As things stand, you are certainly incapable of leaving me and continuing your journey, wherever you are planning to go, alone. Your feet are badly frostbitten.

You couldn't make more than a mile or two. A fresh storm may come up at any time. So, you see — '

'I prefer to be frank and call things by their right name,' the girl retorted.

'Then suppose you answer me two questions frankly. First, your name and where you come from; second, whether Corporal Lafontaine is alive and well.'

'I have said that I can tell you nothing.'

'Then our positions are pretty well defined after all. I must tell you that I am now going out to pick up the trail you took last night, to find out all that is possible. I shall be back early in the afternoon. Please make yourself as comfortable as possible.'

'You are insolent!' she cried, springing to her feet, but wincing with pain as she did so. 'You mean to keep me your prisoner. Very well — I suppose I cannot cross the snows without my snowshoes and without supplies. But at least I ask to be spared a conversation of this character.'

And, with an indignant gesture, she made her way inside the tent. Dan looked after her until the flap had closed. He whistled softly. Then he tightened his belt and thrust his feet into the straps of his snowshoes, and set off down the slope toward the river.

Once on the surface, he had little difficulty in locating the alder patch from which he had retrieved the girl the night before. There the snow still indicated their encounter, though a good deal more had fallen since that time. And Dan began a close examination of the surface, in the endeavor to discover the tracks that the girl had made, and trace them backward.

In this attempt he was completely baffled. For a short distance about the alders Dan could make out the marks of snowshoes, but so much snow had fallen during the night that he quickly realized the attempt must prove a failure. Still, if the girl had come downstream, as he imagined, there ought to be the remains of a campfire nearby.

And for three or four miles Dan went to and fro from bank to bank, examining both the bed of the stream and the higher ground above, but fruitlessly.

In the end he had to confess himself beaten. Whatever indications there might have been lay buried, like her tracks of the previous night, beneath a foot of snow.

Dan covered several more miles, however, before he abandoned hope, making sweeping detours on both sides of the river. At last, when the sun was midway in the west, he started back for his camp.

The dogs greeted him with an outburst of baying. It was almost as if they knew that everything was not quite as it ought to be, and were trying to announce the fact to him. But Dan knew what had happened the moment he reached the little windbreak of willows, for the evidence lay plain enough before his eyes.

Of course the tent was empty. Also, his skis were missing from the sleigh. And the course of the skis, which he had seen as soon as he reached the willows, ran in two more or less parallel lines, straight away from the tent toward the frozen river, and then pointed northward in the direction of Dan's destination. The shallow grooves in the snow showed black in the gray light of the late afternoon, and were visible for a great distance.

Dan looked at the lines and whistled again. The girl was even more resourceful than he had given her the credit of being. She must have lulled his suspicions by assuming a greater incapacity from the frostbite than she was actually suffering. He had thought her helpless without her snowshoes, which she had lost at some time during the night, but what a fool he had been to overlook the skis!

Dan had no doubt that the girl was in some way connected with La Rue.

Something had been in his mind all through the night before he dragged it up to the levels of consciousness, and knew what it was.

When the girl had begun to revive in the tent the night before, she had addressed him by the name of Alphonse. And Alphonse was the name of the prisoner, La Rue.

That she was actually Jehane La Rue, the prisoner's wife, and murderess, Dan dismissed from his mind as incredible. But it was obvious that surprises would be in store for him when he reached the Little Fish.

4

But Dan was fuming with impatience. He had wasted a day, when each day might mean a matter of life or death to Corporal Lafontaine. Hitherto Dan had believed it probable that some accident, or perhaps the scurvy to which Lafontaine had referred in his last report to Headquarters, might have been the cause of the nonappearance of the corporal with his prisoner. But now Dan hardly ventured to hope that Lafontaine was still alive.

He knew, of course, the celerity with which news flies through the vast reaches of the Northland. The whole land, desolate as it is, is a vast whispering gallery. That he was on the way to relieve Lafontaine must have been bruited abroad from the very day he started; there was not a tepee anywhere from the Saskatchewan to the northern ice in which his mission would not have been discussed. And the girl's mysterious appearance, and her evident acquaintance with facts that were as yet concealed from him, made him fear for the worst.

He cursed himself for the folly that had permitted her to escape so readily. But it was no time to lament the past. It was essential now that he should cover the remainder of the journey as swiftly as possible.

It was too late to start that day, but at the earliest dawn Dan was afoot, harnessing the dogs. They were well away before it was light, and though more snow during the night had obliterated the ski tracks, he struck the same general course over the Barrens, which gradually descended toward that cloudy patch on the far horizon which indicated Dan's destination. The sun shone bright by now, but over that distant blur there was no sunlight.

It was the center of the drainage bowl, a region dank with the mist that rose perpetually from the marshes, and shunned like a pestilence by man and beast alike.

Four days later Dan struck the Little Fish, and followed its tortuous course toward the head. The map that he had brought with him was mostly guess-work, or compiled from tradition, since this region was practically unknown. It showed a crude triangle, with Lac Ste. Thérèse as one point, and the shore of the Great Bear another, with the head of the Little Fish as the apex.

The most difficult part of the journey had now begun. Along the scrub-fringed bank of the river ran a rough trail, made perhaps by Indians in the long ago, flying from hostile tribes, and kept open by the few beasts of the Barrens that passed that way. A little distance on the other side of the trail, beyond the fringe of undergrowth, the muskeg began. It bore the weight of the sleigh, but progress was almost impos-sible, for the surface was soft even beneath the snow, while the whole region was dotted with quickmud holes of fathomless depth, as Dan knew, making any attempt to cross it almost certain destruction.

Hence Dan made no attempt to shorten the journey by any quick cuts from point to point of the winding river course, though when the stream bent snakewise upon itself, the temptation was strong. Instead, he forced his way doggedly onward, being often forced to stop and clear a path for dogs and sleigh with the ax through the dense thickets of tangled fern, blueberry shrub, and swamp laurel.

On the night before he expected to arrive at his destination, Dan had flung himself down to rest, exhausted from the labors of an arduous day. He had forced the pace to the utmost in his anxiety to reach Corporal Lafontaine, and in spite of it he had covered less than an average day's march across the Barrens. Sleep descended upon him, dense and stupefying, yet crowded with the phantoms of the past, an unmeaning procession of dream images occasioned probably by the over-exhaustion that kept his brain in activity.

His anxiety for Lafontaine had grown still more acute, too. Each hour of the march had increased his apprehensions for the corporal, and his eagerness to reach the cabin, so that in sleep his mind still pursued the accustomed succession of thoughts, picturing vague disasters.

Then of a sudden the sense of imminent personal danger broke into this dull nightmare, and, half-waking, and not yet realizing where he was, Dan instinctively flung back his head and shoulders. At the same instant the bang of a revolver, almost in his ear, and the acrid stench of powder in his nostrils, brought to him instant realization of his surroundings.

He had felt the wind of the bullet, the powder sting his cheek; the starlight, very faintly illumining the interior of the tent, showed Dan a shadow against the canvas. Dan reacted with the instant automatic response of a man trained to meet such emergencies. A sideward spring from the half-supine position in which he was lying placed in his hand the revolver that had been in his belt beside the sleeping-bag.

The same movement brought him into contact with the wall of the canvas, just as the revolver of the intruder cracked again.

Again the shot missed — and then Dan and the other were struggling in the folds of the tent, while the dogs bayed furiously and strained at the sleigh to which they were fastened.

For a moment Dan thought he had succeeded in grappling the intruder through the canvas. Then they slipped through his fingers, and his struggles only entangled him more thoroughly. To fire was not only contrary to the code of the Police, which reserves the use of the revolver for the last emergency, but was impossible. In the dark, Dan could see nothing. He fought his way free somehow — and then he was himself under the stars, piled among the wrangling, snarling dogs.

He disengaged himself and looked about him for his assailant, but there was no moon, and the terrain, which was a small, open space in the heart of the river scrub, though it formed an excellent windbreak, afforded complete cover for just such a treacherous attack as had been made upon him. Dan had, in fact, selected it only because the alternative had been the muskeg, which was not to be thought of.

Nevertheless, through the volleys of furious baying Dan fancied that he heard a crackling in the bushes some distance down the stream. He crossed the open in three bounds, revolver in hand.

'Halt, or I fire!' he shouted

He heard the crackling again, some distance to the right, and discharged the weapon twice in that direction. But there followed only silence. Pushing his way through the undergrowth, Dan saw the flat level of the illimitable swamps extending before him. But nothing was moving on them, nor, so far as he could see, was there any human figure anywhere.

He raged to and fro along the fringe of the undergrowth. But, as he began to grow cool, he recognized that his assailant had succeeded in effecting his escape. The chances of discovering him were growing momentarily less.

Dan was about to return to the camp when he noticed something lying upon the white level of the snow some distance away, and hurried toward it. He picked it up.

It was a snowshoe. In that fact there was nothing strange. No doubt it had been dropped by his assailant, who had not dared to wait to pick it up.

But it was smaller and more elongated than a man's snowshoe. It was a woman's, and the inference was unmistakable.

And now Dan could see the tracks leading from this point. They ran straight along the fringe of the brush into the distance, and side by side with those of the other snowshoe were the imprints of a small moccasined foot.

If the girl were trying to escape with a single snowshoe, it would not be a difficult matter to overtake her. The imprints of the moccasin sank deep into the snow, which lay soft above the muskeg. He followed the tracks for half a mile along a narrow trail, and down to the ice of the river bed.

And here a surprise awaited him. Outlined distinctly upon the snow-covered surface were the marks of a sleigh and dogs, and among the confused imprints of feet Dan could see the impressions of another pair of snowshoes, this time a man's.

The sleigh had evidently halted at this point to wait while the girl went to Dan's tent upon her murderous mission, for here the tracks ceased. Dan could read the story as well as if it was being reenacted before his eyes. The girl had returned, and the sleigh had turned around and made its journey back toward the point from which it had come.

So far good, but now the reading grew more difficult, for in the faint light it was not easy to disentangle the two sets of tracks, made in the going and returning. It was plain enough to Dan, however, that the girl had been accompanied by a man.

Half a mile further along the stream there was another difficulty. The trail of the girl's snowshoes came down the further bank of the river, indicating that the sleigh must have been waiting for her, and that she had joined it at this point. Dan could see where the dogs had rested.

But — and this was inexplicable — there were also the tracks of the girl's moccasins made on the snow further along the river bed, going both ways.

In other words, the girl seemed to have accompanied the sleigh along the river, and at the same time to have joined it at the point where her single tracks converged down the bank.

Dan scrambled up the bank. He could faintly see the line of tracks across the muskeg. There was no doubt but that the girl had joined the sleigh at that point in the river bed.

He followed the sleigh tracks about a quarter of a mile further. Always there were the double snowshoe tracks, made going and returning.

Then came glare ice, on which the tracks were hopelessly lost, and Dan knew that it would be a waste of time to attempt to pick them up further along. They were not likely to tell him anything more than he had learned already. He turned back toward his camp, stopped for a moment, and regarded the snowshoe that he held with a grim, cynical smile.

'That's what I'd call gratitude,' he said aloud. 'We're going to have a showdown, lady, when we meet again.'

He started on the return journey, but, within a short distance of his camp, he saw something that he had overlooked. At a certain point at the edge of the river the snow was trampled, as if by a number of feet. From the confused impressions it looked very much as if a scuffle had occurred there.

And in the center of the patch something else was lying. It was a hunting knife, not very long, but of razor sharpness. And all along the blade was a sticky, viscid substance. What it was, Dan knew very well.

5

It was anywhere between midnight and morning, but Dan's watch having stopped, he had no present means of gauging the time. In the light of what had occurred, further sleep that night was clearly impossible for him. The discoveries had thrown him into a fever-heat of impatience and speculation. In addition to the risk of renewed attack if he remained where he was, was his eagerness to be in a position to understand who the girl's companion had been, and whom he had been fighting on the bed of the stream. Dan was consumed with impatience to complete the few remaining miles of his journey and clear up the mystery of Lafontaine's silence.

The moon was rising slowly in the east. It would give light enough in a little while, though at present, it was hardly more than a major planet. Dan whipped the protesting dogs into harness with savage vehemence, flung tent and sleeping bag upon the sleigh, and resumed the interminable journey.

A little further on, the thick brush beside the Little Fish dwindled and then gave way to muskeg, which now extended on both sides of the stream near to the brink. The Little Fish itself ran at the bottom of a deepening gorge, over a stony bed, and impetuously enough to prevent ice forming over the rushing torrent in the center. To travel on its surface was therefore an impossibility. However, the muskeg seemed firm enough, though here and there were holes filled with viscid marsh water. It was odd to see water in that bitter cold, but Dan knew that it would tax the strength of the northern winter to freeze those treacherous depths — at least, enough to make travel safe.

He walked ahead, testing the ground and at the same time keeping a lookout for any attempted repetition of the attack on the part of the girl. But the muskeg troubled him more than any anticipation of danger at her hands, for now, as far as Dan could see, the land lay flat as a pancake, unrelieved by any growth except here or there a stunted birch or willow. It would be difficult for even the girl to find ambush anywhere near.

Dan knew the muskeg was treacherous, but he utterly disbelieved the girl's statement that it was impossible to reach the cabin. He believed she was connected with the gang; that they had reappeared, and Lafontaine's presence at the rendezvous seemed to him improbable in the extreme. And yet the consciousness of the imminent danger stirred Dan's heart and quickened his pulses. To match one's wits against the killer, to uphold the law and the repute of the Force in the wildest regions — that was life, to Dan.

Hour after hour he pursued the march while the moon climbed the sky, until the land lay almost as bright as in the day before his eyes. And Dan was nearing the end of his journey. According to the map, the cabin where Lafontaine had trapped La Rue lay at the upper end of the long, narrow lake that had already appeared on his left hand. And now Dan was skirting its borders, only to discover that it contained not water, but muskeg clear to the brim.

This was the very bottom of the bowl, drained from the surrounding mountains. Dan tossed a small boulder upon the quivering surface. It sank slowly, as if into viscid oil, spreading ripples of mud around it. The glassy surface closed over it. And not even snow would lie upon the face of the muskeg. Either it was engulfed or it melted from the warmth generated by the perpetual decomposition and fermentation going on beneath.

Dan shouted to the dogs and running back, swung the gee-pole hard over. The sleigh, which was already teetering upon the brim of the lake, swung around and resumed its journey upon firmer ground.

For perhaps twenty minutes longer, Dan continued the march. Soft as the ground was, he had discovered that it was passable wherever the snow lay deep. Then the head of the lake came into sight, and simultaneously the panorama of Dan's destination unfolded itself in the moonlight.

The spectacle was not in itself remarkable, but it appeared so after the long expanse of monotonous marsh across which Dan had been traveling. The head of the muskeg lake was, in fact, the rim of the bowl. Upon a low ridge of land, fringed with timber of a size that Dan had not seen since he left the timber limits behind him, there stood such a building as he had certainly not expected to discover in that desolate region.

It was an old château, built of logs, and resembling those seigniorial manor houses that are still to be seen in Quebec Province, though on a small scale. All about it was waste land covered with young trees, but evidently from its appearance, the ground was once cleared. And at the head of the lake, separated from the château by a strip of muskeg perhaps three hundred yards in width and surrounded by the same bog, was a small island.

It was not more than about an acre in extent, its boundaries clearly defined in the moonlight. On this, in the midst of a growth of smaller timber, was a great mass of stone, perhaps the size of a large house and about as high. It was one of those outcroppings of limestone that are not infrequently found in that country where at some time in past ages a landslide has displaced the accumulated debris of ages, and disclosed the basic rock.

At the foot of this mass of stone was a long, low structure built also of logs, and looking like a trading store.

Château and trading store faced each other across that rim of bog, and it was evident that at some time in the past they had been intimately associated with one another.

The trading store, according to the directions that Dan had received, marked the end of his journey. A quarter of a mile further, and he would know whether Lafontaine was alive or dead.

He cracked the whip, and the dogs, as if they understood that the toil of the long journey was almost over, strained against their breast-straps. For a few moments the sleigh bounded over the snow. Then it began to drag, went on a little way, and stopped. Dan saw that there was no longer snow beneath it.

The utmost efforts of the animals were unable to budge it. And they were mired to the knees.

Then Dan discovered that he himself was already ankle-deep in the soft bog. Almost imperceptibly it was sucking him down, closing softly about his feet, his legs.

Man and dogs were alike trapped in the maw of the dreaded muskeg!

At first Dan fought desperately to free himself from the trap. To pull his legs free was not difficult, for the swamp was soft and yielding, but as fast as he freed one foot the other sank deeper in, and every step forward meant a renewal of the struggle. The dogs, now belly deep in the mire, were howling piteously and making frantic efforts to escape in vain. With a mighty effort, Dan forced his way to their head. Grabbing Miska, the leader, he tugged with all his strength.

He pulled her bodily from the swamp, only to find that he was now stuck fast to the knees, and as the terrified beast hurled herself against her harness, she began to sink again. Glancing back along the line, Dan saw that the fifth dog was already buried to the haunches.

And that was the beginning of a desperate, hideous struggle for life that was to be a nightmare to Dan long afterward, both in his waking and his sleeping hours. Grimly he set himself to such a battle as he had never dreamed of, there beneath the brilliant moon-light.

In the face of the great terror, the dogs became what they had been not many generations back. They snarled and bit and fought one another, and as each one went down those that were not so deeply trapped tore at its throat, and tore at each other as they fought over their prey. It was not hunger — it was the life instinct at war with death; the same that makes wolves fall upon their slain companions and rend them. And in the midst of the snarling tangle Dan fought like a madman, a hopeless struggle destined to failure from the first.

Not the least terror of that nightmare was the look in Miska's eyes as she went under. Between man and dog there had sprung up one of those not rare affections that the trapper knows; Miska alone had seemed to retain the dog nature to the end.

In the horror of the disaster Dan had

almost forgotten that he, too, was trapped. As the quivering, jelly-like surface closed over the last dog, he came to the realization that he was lying prone on his face, and that his knees and thighs and shoulders were slowly sinking.

Behind him was the sleigh, now nothing but a flat board upon the surface of the swamp. There was something grotesque in the sight of the supplies gradually descending into the ground.

Dan flung himself free after a fight with the swamp, as if it had been a human antagonist. He squirmed across the mud to the side of the sleigh, and threw off the supplies. They sank almost as quickly as the boulders that he had thrown into the viscid lake.

And Dan's last battle for life was of the same tragic grotesque character. Freed of the weight of its burden, the surface of the sleigh became a flat board resting on the muskeg, and in part upborne by it. The pull of the buried beasts was slowly tilting it downward at the forward end. Dan threw his weight upon the rear as a counterbalance. And for what seemed an infinity, the struggle between man and swamp went on, the muskeg sucking downward and Dan forcing up the front of the surface by hurling his full weight upon the back.

The sweat streamed down his face as his strength was leaving him; encased in viscid mud from head to foot, he fought there under the brilliant moon, which was slowly losing brilliance as the first light of dawn began to creep over the swamp.

Dan was becoming unconscious, his struggle growing mechanical; by degrees, as the dead beasts sank still deeper into the fathomless maw of the mud, Dan was no longer able to counterbalance their weight. Of a sudden the sucking swamp closed in.

Dan found himself the sole thing on the face of the marsh which, like a spongy mass, was rising round him.

And once again, with a last effort, he succeeded in fighting himself free.

A score of yards away was safety — and he could not have moved a score of inches.

But as he raised his eyes, looking back hopelessly, he heard a cry and saw a figure standing in a tiny windbreak of willow saplings with a sleigh and three dogs, strung out black under the moon behind it.

Over the face of the marsh like a huge snake, a rope came streaking. But of the finale of that grim struggle, Dan never remembered anything thereafter. One mental picture was of himself battling against the swamp, prone on the ground; the next was of his lying on the snow with firm soil underneath him, clutching the rope, which was bending one of the saplings to the roots, and looking up into the face of an old Indian.

6

Into that Gethsemane of physical anguish Dan had flung the last ounce of his strength. He was dimly conscious of being lifted upon the sleigh and being drawn away. The idea hazily crossed his mind that this was the man who had accompanied the girl along the river bed when she came to him upon her murderous errand. But though he knew himself to be completely in the Indian's power, and might be on his way to his death, Dan was powerless to move hand or foot.

Nor did he greatly care. The tragedy in the muskeg had for the time broken his spirit, even as it had broken his body. And the affair had been the culmination of days of struggle to reach Lafontaine, which had taxed his powers of resistance to the utmost.

It was a complete physical collapse.

Even when the movements of the sleigh stopped, and Dan felt himself being carried into a warm and comfortable interior, he could not arouse himself from his torpor. Unconsciousness became complete. At length he opened his eyes to find himself in such strange surroundings that he started up, bewildered, and groping through a haze of confused memories before he realized that he must be in the château that he had seen from the other side of the muskeg.

It was midday, to judge from the appearance of the sun which, some distance above the horizon, was casting long slanting rays of light into the room. Dan had been lying upon a mattress, placed in front of a large stove that diffused a comfortable warmth through the long interior.

But the amazing thing was that interior. The long hall was furnished with chairs and tables that must have been transported by sleigh from some point hundreds of miles distant. There were well-tanned skins for rugs, and there were even two or three pictures on the well-fitted boards of the walls which again, must have been brought from some lumber mill. Everything seemed to indicate that this was the home of persons of breeding and refinement.

And yet there was an atmosphere of decrepitude about the interior, too. Dan could see that there was mold here and there, as if the house had long been in disuse. Old cobwebs hung from the rafters; there was the smell of long-closed houses in the air. It was like the ghost of an old seigniorial manor house momentarily reincarnated.

As Dan started up, his memories rushing back to him, the Indian came through the doorway. A very old man, with a deeply wrinkled, impassive face and snow-white hair, he moved softly toward Dan, watching him very intently.

'You are feeling better, Monsieur?' he asked in French.

'I'm feeling all right. Where am I?'

'In the château on the edge of Lac Sec (Dry Lake), Monsieur.'

Dan strode to the window and looked out. He could see the mass of limestone on the island, apparently no more than two hundred yards across the muskeg arm, but the cabin itself was hidden among the trees.

'Is Corporal Lafontaine over there?' asked Dan, pointing.

'I do not know, Monsieur.'

'You don't know? Is anyone there? A policeman — with a prisoner?'

'I do not know, Monsieur,' repeated the Indian stolidly.

Dan could get nothing more out of him than that. He had already discovered that his revolver was gone, but whether the Indian had deprived him of it or whether it had fallen from his holster during struggles in the muskeg, it was impossible to know.

'Who lives here?'

'It is Mademoiselle Camille, Monsieur.'

'I wish to see her.'

'She wishes to see you, Monsieur, but she has had to go away.'

'When will she be back?'

'I do not know, Monsieur. Perhaps by nightfall.'

'Who else lives here?'

'There is nobody else, Monsieur.'

Dan was growing more bewildered. Who was this girl living here alone? That she could be the girl who had tried to murder him in his tent was, of course, unthinkable; and yet — Dan tried to puzzle it out, but the entire situation was unthinkable too, and there was the matter of Lafontaine, which would brook no delay.

'Tell mademoiselle that I thank her for her hospitality,' said Dan. 'And I realize that I owe my life to you also. I am going to the cabin at the head of the lake. I shall return by evening to pay my respects to mademoiselle.'

'There is no way to the cabin, Monsieur.'

'But there must be a way. How could that cabin have been built if there is no means of access?'

'There is no way, Monsieur,' repeated the Indian in his stolid manner.

'I'm going to find a way,' answered Dan.

He stepped out of the château. He had half suspected that the Indian would attempt to offer some resistance, but nothing of the sort seemed to be in the old man's mind, and, refusing to burden his mind with any further speculations in the fact of the one task that lay before him, Dan made his way down the slope of the little plateau toward the edge of the muskeg.

The rim of the bowl was quite clearly defined. Into this sink for centuries uncounted all the drainage of the great waterways had been carrying down the muck that filled it, so that it resembled a great pit constructed by nature to hold the billions of tons of vegetable refuse that reached to the brim of it, with solid earth about it. It was a veritable lake, a sluggishly moving stream of mire, overflowing at the farther end into the swamps that covered thousands of square miles of territory. Dan could see the little island in front of him, hardly more than a stone's throw away, with the great mass of limestone and the cabin among the trees, but even without the Indian's warning it was obvious that he could not hope to set foot on that moving river of muskeg.

He tossed a stone upon its surface, and it sank immediately, as if in a thick, viscid oil. The whole surface quivered, stirred, and slowly subsided.

Dan made his way along the edge of the swamp to a point immediately opposite the head of the lake. Here, where the cabin was invisible, and the island seemed no more than a hundred yards away, he believed there must be some way of approach.

But again each stone that he tossed

into the swamp sank immediately. And for two or three hours Dan moved to and fro, repeating his experiment within a half-circle about the lake-head, but always with the same result.

The sun was dipping into the horizon when he found himself compelled to abandon the attempt as hopeless. Certainly at one time the muskeg had been bridged, but he realized that it would be a matter of weeks, if not months, to discover the way. Unless there came a spell of such bitter weather as would freeze the treacherous surface hard, and of that there was at present no sign at all. The problem seemed insurmountable.

Fuming with anger, Dan returned to the château. The Indian had already prepared his evening meal: caribou haunch and amazing coffee. Dan found that he was ravenous. It was not until he had satisfied his appetite that he attempted to question the old man again.

'Mademoiselle Camille?' he asked.

'She awaits you, Monsieur. If you will come this way . . . '

With a sense of stupefaction Dan followed the Indian through a doorway at the further end of the long hall into another room.

It was almost as large as the hall, but furnished in a still more amazing way. On the floor was a carpet, faded and threadbare, but of a kind that Dan had never seen north of Edmonton. The chairs and tables were of carved wood, the lounge was covered with velour, and on the walls were three or four portraits of men and women, in peruke and military uniforms, in hoops and brocade.

And yet there was the same air of desolation and neglect about the place, as if it had been long closed and abandoned, as if its past had been revived only for the immediate purpose of weaving itself into his own story.

Standing in the center of the room, under a big hanging lamp, Dan saw the girl!

Dan, looking at her, for the life of him could think of nothing to say to her. He realized that it was by her desire that the old Indian had saved him from death in the muskeg. Death and life seemed to have been tossed from one to the other of them as one tosses a ball, and here they two stood, face to face once more.

But the girl seemed equally at a loss, though she had arranged the interview, and she stood staring at him, a look of haggard wretchedness upon her face.

'Well, we're quits,' said Dan at length. 'You tried to murder me, and now you've saved me from a worse kind of death. I don't quite get the point of it all, but I suppose it has some meaning to you.'

'Yes, we're quits,' answered the girl. 'You saved my life, and I've saved yours. We owe each other nothing. Perhaps I felt that we had to even up the score before we could stand in our true relationship toward each other as enemies. But — well, my emotions don't matter. Women change quickly, don't they? I want to know what you are going to do.'

'I'll tell you what I'm going to do,' said Dan. 'I'm going to cross that strip of muskeg and find out what has happened to Corporal Lafontaine. I'm not under any delusion that he's still alive. But I mean to learn what his fate has been. Then I shall come back. I shall learn who you are, and what your part has been in this business. And then I shall bring back La Rue and anyone else who is wanted by the law. Did you suppose I meant to abandon my task?'

'You would have abandoned it forever if I hadn't had Louis drag you from the muskeg,' the girl retorted, a spot of vivid red appearing on either cheek. 'There is no way to that deserted cabin. You can go no further.'

'*Listen to me!*' Dan felt a sudden flaming anger seize him. 'I've lost my dogs, everything — Miska, the best dog I've ever known. You chose to drag me from this devilish swamp. Your motives are known to yourself. *But I'm going to that cabin.*'

And Dan felt his eyes grow moist as he thought of that last look Miska had given him. As the muskeg closed over her head she had tried to lick his hands.

'I wish I'd let you die! I wish I'd killed you in your tent!' cried the girl passionately. 'I have told you again and again that there's no way over the swamps. That cabin was built before the landslide, twenty years ago.'

'But there is a way, and you know what it is,' Dan answered. 'You're going to guide me there, and you are going to put me on the trail of Alphonse La Rue. I don't know whether you are his wife or not, but I know that you are shielding him, and I believe that Lafontaine has been murdered as Corporal Anderson was murdered.'

'Alphonse La Rue?' cried the girl violently. 'I told you you were mad. Don't you know that Alphonse La Rue is dead? He died last autumn.'

'Your first admission — whether true

74

or false,' answered Dan, and again he saw those spots of vivid red flame on the girl's cheeks. 'Then you can also tell me as to the fate of Lafontaine. And you're going to answer me. If those wretches have killed him — '

'He's in that cabin,' answered the girl sullenly.

'Over there? Alive?'

'Of course he's alive. Policemen have as many lives as cats, haven't they?'

'Is he maimed? Disabled? No? Then what is he doing there now that La Rue is — as you say — dead? Why is he waiting there? I mean to have the truth.'

'He's been waiting for the muskeg to freeze over. He's been waiting there since the spring, like Napoleon on a little St. Helena, and I've been watching him from here. That's funny, isn't it? He got in in the very cold weather last March, and trapped La Rue there. It was clever and daring of him, I grant him that. But he'll have to wait for colder weather than we're having now before he gets out again!'

Dan continued staring at her. Everything that the girl was saying to him seemed a tissue of lies. Suddenly his eyes fell upon her arm, which she had been holding close to her side, under the cloak she had about her shoulders, and he perceived that there was a bandage around it. The underside of the bandage was stained with blood. Dan recalled the blood-stained knife that he had found. And that was evidence enough that she was the woman who had been in his tent, even if the snowshoes had not also pointed to her. Probably it was the Indian, Louis, who had tried to dissuade her from her murderous project, and grappled with her for the knife. Who was she? Jehane La Rue? Who else could she be?

'Listen to me,' he said grimly, 'You tell me that Corporal Lafontaine has been in that cabin for months, waiting for the muskeg to freeze, and that you have been watching him from here and gloating over his sufferings. Probably you know that he has been suffering from scurvy. Well, I'm going to pay you a compliment by saying that I believe you.'

'How dare you!'

Dan smiled. 'I'm taking you at your word as to that. But I know there is a way across the muskeg, and you're going to take me there.'

'You're threatening me?'

'Exactly. You're going to take me there.'

'I know one way. I'm willing to show you that.'

'Which way?'

'The way *in!*' she cried triumphantly. 'Not the way *out.* I'll *never* show him the way out, or you *either.* I'll take you *in*, and you can join him there. Two members of the police trapped on an island in the muskeg! It will make a pretty story, won't it?' She began laughing, a sort of spasmodic choking that was almost hysteria. 'I mean,' she cried, with a sudden, violent gesture, 'that Corporal Lafontaine could have saved the life of Alphonse La Rue when he was dying of scurvy, if he had agreed to let him go. He let him die instead.'

'What was Alphonse La Rue to you?' asked Dan.

'*He was my husband!*'

7

Dan remained staring at her without uttering a word. So this girl *was* Jehane La Rue, as he had suspected from the beginning! No, not suspected — known!

She could not have been anyone else. He had let his mind trick him into the pretense that she might be someone else, but he had known from the first that, as soon as the problem of La Rue and Lafontaine was settled he would have to recognize her for who she was, and — act upon his instructions.

And thus everything became clear to him — her warning, her attempt upon his life, and the reaction of remorse, in which she had saved him from the muskeg, probably in the hope of being able to drive some bargain with him.

She was not utterly base, then. And for those few moments during which

Dan continued staring at her, he was conscious of an odd sense of pity for this girl. And this was mingled with a feeling of horror that such a girl as that should be the wife of the notorious outlaw, the cruelest, vilest man who had ever ranged through the North; and that she should herself be wanted by the Police upon the charge of murder.

A capital charge! And Canadian law knows no sentimentality. Dan knew as he stood there, looking into her face, which had grown misty, that she was destined to hang for the murder of young Anderson. She would hang, a shapeless, masked thing, with a rope around her neck, in some grim prison yard, and the repulsive thought filled him with pity that she must inevitably come to such an end.

Pity, not only for this girl, but for every man whom he had ever in the past caught in the meshes of the law.

For the first time in his career Sergeant Dan Keane questioned the value of his calling. But it was only for a few moments. Then came the revulsion. The thoughts of young Anderson, a boy of twenty-two whom he had known, foully stabbed to death by this woman while he slept; the thought of the murdered factor and the crimes that had filled the Northland with terror — crimes with which Jehane La Rue's name was linked as well as that of her husband — came as a healthy reagent. It was perhaps the episode of the preceding day that had momentarily shaken the strong soul of the man. Dan became himself again.

And, looking into the girl's face, he was conscious of no pity for her. Rather she seemed like some hideous thing in a beautiful human body that he must destroy. And would destroy, gladly, in the light of his duty.

But he realized that the girl had been reading more or less all of what had passed in his mind.

'You have a warrant for my arrest, Sergeant Keane?' she said quietly.

'I have,' Dan answered. He had

suspected from the beginning that the warrant, secretly though it had been prepared, was known to that ramifying underworld that was in touch with the Police posts everywhere.

'The fact that I have just saved your life means nothing at all to you?'

'So far as my duty is concerned — nothing at all. No more than the fact that you tried to murder me a few hours before.'

'Ah, you policemen. You are splendid, magnificent — machines! But still, sometimes in the course of your duty you find it necessary to make a bargain?'

'What bargain?'

'This. Whom do you want more? Myself or my — husband?'

'Both,' answered Dan simply. 'When I return, it will be with both of you.' The question puzzled him a little, even bothered him. Surely the woman understood that he was not open to any such bargain as the one she had seemed to suggest — that he should let her go

82

in return for Alphonse La Rue, who she had said was dead.

Besides, if Lafontaine really had La Rue —

'What I mean is this. If I show you the way across the muskeg — the way in, mind you, not out; if you are blindfolded and led in by me, will you agree to let me go, find your own way out, and — capture me later?'

Dan reflected. It was not the sort of proposition that made any sort of appeal to him. But if he refused, Jehane La Rue would mean nothing unless he first relieved Lafontaine, or captured La Rue, in case Lafontaine was dead.

Lafontaine's fate must be cleared up. Dan did not believe a word of what the girl had been saying to him. He could see that she was desperate, willing to forswear herself, do anything to circumvent him.

'I agree to that proposal,' answered Dan, after a moment of hesitation.

'You swear not to try to detain me until you have been to the island? Upon your honor as a policeman?'

'I swear it.'

'Nor to remove the blindfold? Very well, I'll take you there as soon as it grows light.'

Impatient as he was, Dan had to rest content with that. He lay down to rest again in the long hall. He did not know where Jehane — whom the Indian had called Camille — had gone. It was no use trying to watch the front entrance of the building, for there might be a dozen ways of egress. It was highly probable, Dan reflected, that the girl was even now engaged in a murder plot more efficaciously conceived than the one which he had frustrated the night before. And he had no revolver. Still, there was nothing to do but go on. At last he was going to know the truth.

That was the last thought that passed through his mind before he dropped asleep, convinced that the subconscious would arouse him in time in case any danger threatened him. Yet when he started up hearing his name spoken, the

Indian, Louis, was already at his side.

'Monsieur, Mademoiselle Camille is waiting for you outside the château.'

'Tell Madame La Rue that I'll be with her in a few moments,' answered Dan with emphasis.

For an instant he thought he saw a flicker of emotion in the impassive face of the Indian, but it was succeeded instantly by the same stolid mask. Dan fastened his belt and went out into the dawn.

Jehane La Rue was waiting just outside the building.

'Well, Monsieur Keane, I am here,' she said, 'trusting in the honor of a policeman, as you see. Permit me to fasten the handkerchief.'

She had a dark silk cloth in her hand. Standing on tiptoe, she began fastening it about Dan's forehead. He felt her fingertips about his eyes and in his hair. Then he was standing beside her in darkness.

'Come, Monsieur, permit me to guide you.'

Dan expected her to cross the muskeg arm; instead, he could discern that she was taking him around the head of the lake. It was evident that there was no way across that narrow strip, where it might be presumed the swamp, being deepest, was always impassable. As he moved, Dan kept his hearing strained for any sounds that might be indicative of a treacherous attack, but he heard nothing.

With the girl guiding him, Dan moved forward. Sometimes she would utter a brief warning as to a tree in the way, but for the most part they walked in silence until Dan estimated that half an hour had elapsed; then the girl stopped.

'You can take off the handkerchief now, Sergeant Keane,' she said briskly.

Dan removed it and handed it to her. During the half-hour that they had been traveling the day had broken.

Dan discovered, as he had thought, that they had circled the head of the lake; they were actually upon the extreme point of the island, with the mass of rock looming in front of them, and the muskeg swamps behind.

'You are satisfied that I have kept my word, as you have kept yours?' asked the girl.

And, without waiting for Dan's answer she broke away and began running back over the muskeg. Dan watched the course she took, but it was impossible to draw any deductions from it. Surefooted, she seemed to skim the treacherous surface almost like a bird. In a minute or two she had disappeared among the trees.

Dan turned again. Who was within the cabin: La Rue, or Lafontaine? Was La Rue alive or dead? The girl had said both. Would his approach be greeted with a fusillade from the murderous outlaw, concealed behind some loophole?

Dan thought the latter possibility about the strongest. And those few moments of his advance toward the rock were the culmination of all the suspense that he had endured through-out the journey. In front of him the round orb of the sun appeared a blood-red rim above the surface of the swamp. In a minute more he would know, in a minute more he would know — in a few seconds more, Dan kept telling himself.

He was in the open now, past the trees, and expecting every moment to feel the shock of bullets.

Then the figure of a man appeared in the entrance of the hut, a short and rather swarthy man, wearing the King's scarlet!

8

'You're Sergeant Keane? I heard you were on your way, though I'm trapped in here. You'll think that strange, but — '

'Corporal Lafontaine, of course? I'm — I'm mighty glad I've found you, Lafontaine.' Dan found it a little difficult to keep his voice under control as he gazed for the first time into the face of the famous hunter of men. The corporal seemed very voluble, but who wouldn't be under such circumstances? 'I was afraid I'd be too late.'

'Nothing like that,' replied the other, speaking with a strong French accent, but in a by no means unmelodious voice. 'I've been here since spring. La Rue was dying for weeks, and I didn't know when I came in that it was by a freak, that this damned muskeg only freezes in the coldest weather. That freak's what got La Rue. How the devil did you make it, Keane? I tried only yesterday, and got stuck to the waist. Did you see Jehane La Rue? She came to the edge of the muskeg and shouted to me that you were on your way, but you'd never reach me. And I couldn't get my hands on her. Why, old man, you look as if you've been up to the neck yourself! Come in and get cleaned up, and we'll talk things over after . . . '

Dan gathered, from Lafontaine's volubility, that the corporal was slightly unhinged after his experiences alone upon the island. He accompanied him inside the long building. The place had been, as Dan had thought, a trading store at one time, but the long counter was gone, and there was a large table, with chairs, and three or four camp beds. It looked as if this had been the headquarters of La Rue and his gang, and it would have been difficult for them to have found a safer one.

Dan cleaned some of the mud off his uniform, and put on some clothes that the other gave him while his own clothes were drying. Breakfast was quickly prepared by his host. It consisted of bread and stewed rabbit.

'How did you get the rabbit, Lafontaine?' Dan asked.

'Wire snares. I'll tell you about those rabbits later, Keane. You'll never run short of rabbits long as you're here. God, I'm sick of rabbit! I've lived on it since summer. Did you meet the La Rue woman?'

Dan told him briefly that he had made her act as his guide. He did not feel like being confidential with Lafontaine. He was becoming more convinced that Lafontaine was a little unbalanced, principally from the disconnected way in which he talked. Dan, studying him closely as they ate, concluded that he must have suffered severely.

He was disappointed in Lafontaine. He knew that for years past the famous little corporal had been on lonely trails in quest of very many wanted men.

Decidedly any barracks polish that he had acquired in the beginning would have worn off. Still, Lafontaine was lacking in something — and Dan was trying to figure out what that something was when the corporal rose.

'Want to see La Rue?' he asked.

'You've got his body still?'

'Sure enough! Everything was frozen stiff when he died at the end of October.'

However, Dan asked no questions, but accompanied the other out of the door. The Frenchman led the way toward the great mass of limestone, which Dan now saw, was seamed with fissures, as such masses usually are. He squeezed his body through one of these crevices in the other's wake.

Dan found himself in a little hollow vault, about the dimensions of a small hall bedroom. Stalactites hung from the walls, with small stalagmites beneath and the sun's rays, throwing a narrow beam of light through the narrow entrance, banded them with prismatic hues.

The effect was indescribably beautiful. Now blue, now green, now gold, now red; the stalactites glittered like colored ice. Yet it was ghastly too, for the little place was like a mortuary chapel. Although the stretcher cot on which the body of the dead man was lying occupied almost the entire length of one side of the cave, for a moment or two, owing to some ocular trick, or his bewilderment at the sheer beauty of the scene, Dan failed to perceive it.

Then he saw it, behind a hanging fringe of stalactites. They drooped over the cot, reflecting the colored hues upon the face of the dead man. He lay upon his back, the arms folded across the breast. The body was, of course, frozen stiff, and it did not appear to have suffered any of the change of mortality.

Clothed in a mackinaw and heavy trousers, it lay there, a placid expression upon the hollow face, wax-white save where the bands of light lay across it. Whatever La Rue's life had been, death seemed to have invested his features with a singular dignity, almost nobility, as it invests those of so many.

And except for the hollowness of the cheeks, and the emaciation of the face, Dan could see no signs that La Rue had died of scurvy. He bent over the body, examining it closely, but without touching it. As he did so, the other took a step forward.

'I'd keep away from it,' he said with a nervous laugh. 'I mean there might be danger — what I mean is, I suppose it was scurvy we were suffering from but I'm no doctor. It might have been something else.'

'It might have been,' responded Dan placidly. Nevertheless, he stepped back from the stretcher. 'You both had scurvy badly, did you?' he asked.

'Yes, all the summer. I tell you we were in a pretty bad way. If there had been any means of saving him I'd have given my hand to have saved his life.

But he just got worse from day to day.'

'And you — recovered!'

'Yes, I'll tell you all about that. Let's get out of here. I suppose we'll have to take him down to be identified?'

'We'll talk that over later,' answered Dan, following his companion out into the pale sunlight. The Frenchman led the way back into the large room, looking over his shoulder with an anxious expression two or three times, as if to make sure that Dan was following him. He closed the door, and they sat down at the table again.

The Frenchman leaned forward confidentially. 'Say, Keane,' he began, 'I may as well tell you some good news. I came upon some of the private stock of the La Rue gang.' A sort of nervous, chuckling laugh came from his lips. 'I'm not referring to the rotten hooch La Rue gave the Indians for their furs, but his own private brand. In fact, La Rue put me wise to the cache where it was hidden. We managed to get through the summer on it somehow, and there's still a little left. Now how would a little drink feel to you? Not a Prohibition-ist, are you, Keane?'

'Not in principle — only in practice,' answered Dan. 'The fact is I never drink in Prohibition territory. I like keeping the laws that I'm paid to help enforce. But that's only a personal prejudice of mine. If you want a drink, I guess I won't be called upon to report it at Headquarters.'

'For which much thanks,' responded the other with a curt laugh. 'God, man, if you'd been shut up with a prisoner all summer, having to watch every move he made, and both of you sick with scurvy, I guess you wouldn't feel so straight-laced about it. Well, I'll take you at your word, Keane.'

He crossed the room and took down a bottle from a shelf, pouring out a liberal drink into a tin mug. Dan noticed that there was a fine tremor of the fingers as he did so. He came back and sat down, draining off the contents.

Meanwhile Dan had not uttered a word.

'Well, you want the history of this business, I suppose,' said the Frenchman. 'As you know, a party of us set out something over a year ago, and we got on the trail of La Rue and that gang of his. That crowd had certainly been playing merry hell up in these parts. The Indians were terrorized for hundreds of miles around. Well, we didn't get them, and we didn't find that cache of furs they stole after murdering the factor up at White's Point on the Mackenzie. But we dispersed the gang. The rest went back, but I stayed on the job. I had a hunch that I could get La Rue.'

The liquor had already loosened the Frenchman's tongue; the man was gesticulating and talking loosely, tripping over the syllables. Dan, sitting opposite him at the table, was gathering his impressions by the eye rather than by the ear.

'I had a hunch that I could get La

Rue, who was the brains of the gang. I knew he'd married that Desmoulins girl. Old Desmoulins built this store, you know, before the landslide came down and cut it off from his château over there. He was a Frenchman of the old school, with crazy feudal ideas, and he wanted to carve a seigniory out of this district. Well, as I was saying, La Rue married the Desmoulins girl, and there wasn't a trick he knew that she couldn't go him one better, after a while. I trailed her, found this hangout, and trapped La Rue here last winter.

'You remember how bitter cold it was in March. The muskeg froze, and that's something that happens only once in five years or so. The gang knew the way, but I've never found it. I blundered in like a fool, without guessing what I was up against. But I guess you and I can find the way out easy enough, or maybe you've got on the right side of La Rue's woman, eh, old man?'

'Go on with the story,' answered Dan.

The other started. 'The story? Why — that's all. I got La Rue easy enough, but I've been here nine months, and nearly lost my life trying to get out. And the La Rue woman got in one night and tried to knife me. Say, old man, I'm going to get another drink.'

Dan watched his every movement as he got the bottle down from the shelf and helped himself again. He filled the mug half full and drained it. Now his manner seemed to have undergone a change. He was still more loquacious, and yet with a sub-note of sullenness and suspicion.

He flopped down in the chair. 'Well, I guess that about covers everything, Keane,' he said. 'Now let me ask you about — '

'Wait a little. How about that scurvy? How did it happen that you got well and La Rue died?'

'Why, La Rue and I both had it, but he had it worse than me, because he got drunk on that hooch every night at first. I wouldn't touch it till I was left alone.

Still, I didn't feel it was up to me to stop him taking a drink when he wanted one. It was all he had to live for. There was plenty of flour that the gang had left in the cache, along with the whisky, but there was absolutely nothing else — not even a bag of potatoes or compressed vegetables. We couldn't get out of this damn place to hunt our meat. We lived on flour and whisky till I remembered something I'd read about snaring rabbits with a bit of wire.

'I was going to tell you about the rabbits. The island's swarming with them. You see, there are wolves around here, and when they chase the rabbits — why, the rabbits can cross the muskeg where the wolves can't. So they come here. You hear them all night long — patter, patter, when the wolves are after them. Yes, I'll never want to look a rabbit in the face again after I get out of here.

'Well, I soon got onto the snaring trick and that saved me, but La Rue was too far gone. He died at the beginning of the winter, and I've been here alone two months now, with that crazy woman flitting about outside. I've been thinking of snaring her.' He laughed unsteadily. 'If the muskeg don't freeze soon, I guess we're in for another year of it, living on rabbits. Why do you suppose the La Rue woman let you in?'

Again, Dan left the question unanswered. 'There's one thing I'd like to ask, Lafontaine,' he said. 'How did you hold La Rue?'

'Why, I slipped the cuffs on him every night.'

'Where do you keep them?'

But Dan's eyes had already followed the other's involuntary glance toward the shelf overhead, where he saw the irons.

'What's worrying you?' the Frenchman snarled suddenly.

'Well, you see,' answered Dan, 'I've been trying to figure out, if what you've been telling me's correct, how it happens that my skis are standing there against the door.'

'Your skis?'

'Exactly. You see, Madame La Rue borrowed them from my sleigh one day to leave in a hurry. There's no question but those are my skis; however, if you don't want to take my word for it, look at the leather on the right one, and you'll see that it's been ripped and sewed up with *babiche*.'

'What the — what you mean to — ?'

'Pretty clear evidence that Madame La Rue has been in this cabin lately, friend. Sit down, La Rue, and hold your hands — '

The lightning leap the other made did not catch Dan napping. Before he could draw the revolver from its holster Dan had overturned the table, and came crashing down upon him with it. A brief struggle, and the weapon was in Dan's hand.

'Get up, La Rue,' he said. 'You might have thought out a better story than that. Or you'd have done better to have tried to get away instead of trusting to those brains of yours to fool me. You see,' he added, 'I saw the bullet hole in poor Lafontaine's head, under the hair, behind the ear. Just reach me down those handcuffs!'

9

Dan had heard many strange stories about about his prisoner, but the reality surpassed them. His first outburst of malignant rage ended, La Rue submitted to being handcuffed quietly enough, and relieved of his revolver and a knife as long as a poniard, which, being hidden in his sleeve, Dan nearly overlooked. La Rue's rage was, however, vented chiefly against Jehane.

It was Dan who spoke of her, telling La Rue — as he thought it right to do — that he held a warrant for her arrest on the charge of murdering Anderson. As it was impossible for him to take in two prisoners at the same time, particularly when one of them was a woman, Dan proposed to take La Rue first to the nearest post on the Mackenzie, returning for his wife after.

'You're mighty sure of getting her,

aren't you, Sergeant?' sneered the Frenchman. 'Damn her, I told her the trick wouldn't work, but I let myself be persuaded.'

'Just what was the idea, La Rue?' Dan asked.

'The idea? Just to get you out of the way instead of killing off another policeman. It happened to suit me, that's the reason.'

'I guess you trusted too much to those brains of yours,' said Dan. 'Hell, if it hadn't been for that bullet hole in Lafontaine's head, you might have got away with it. Didn't know the skin stretches after death, did you, La Rue? You all slip up in one way or another.'

He was encouraging La Rue to talk, in the hope of picking up some further information, though the murder of Lafontaine had filled him with bitter hatred for the murderer. He asked him how he got the corporal.

La Rue burst into a fit of laughter. 'Lafontaine was dead easy, even for a policeman,' he grinned. 'But it wasn't me who got him, it was Jehane.'

Dan felt sick with horror, no less at La Rue's incrimination of his wife than at the thought of it. Dan was sure of one thing, and that was that there was still a good deal to be cleared up in respect of the motives of Jehane La Rue.

'Easy, *dead easy*,' La Rue went on, grinning broadly. 'She crossed the muskeg and got him while he was asleep. Even Lafontaine had to sleep sometimes. He nearly caught her once. He knew she'd get him in the end, though, and the last week of his life he had the horrors. And that's the way she's going to get you,' he added malignantly.

Dan was beginning to understand his prisoner's motives in hiding there instead of making a break for freedom. Undeniably he was safer there than he would be if he showed his face at any post along any of the trails. And while La Rue was of course acquainted with the secret of the passage across the muskeg, all he had had to do was to sit still and behave like a model prisoner until Jehane 'got' Lafontaine. Unless, then, Dan could himself solve that secret, or unless the weather grew cold enough to freeze the surface of the bog, he might kick his heels there indefinitely.

And then some night — some night when his watch relaxed, as it must inevitably — Jehane La Rue would come creeping across the swamp, knife or revolver in her hand, and he would be in danger of going the way that Lafontaine had gone.

The prospect was not a pleasant one, and Dan determined to maintain his watchfulness as long as he and his prisoner were there. That night he fastened La Rue firmly with a rope, as well as handcuffing him, in such a way that he could move with fair freedom on his bed, but would be comparatively helpless. He carefully searched the interior of the place for weapons, and for anything that could be used as an implement of offense. He barred the door, which was fortified with great bolts. As for the window, it was double — the gang had certainly known how to make themselves snug — and strongly nailed inside and out. Dan was at last convinced that it was impossible either for La Rue to attack him while he slept, or for *anyone* to gain ingress without awakening him.

As for himself, he would have to sleep like the seal, in twenty-second snatches. But Dan was more or less habituated to watchful sleep.

There was a pile of swamp logs outside the cabin, drawn from the muskeg. Dan had noticed that logs were imbedded in it everywhere, carried down from the forest limits through centuries by the irresistible movement of the slow tide. When the stove was ablaze, Dan felt more comfortable. The shock of Lafontaine's murder was beginning to pass. Horrible as his death had been, the little corporal had passed as he would have wished, perhaps, to pass. And he got his man. And Dan was holding him.

La Rue had watched all Dan's preparations with a malicious grin that seemed to hint at some card he held in reserve.

'You're taking a lot of trouble to keep alive, Keane, aren't you?' he drawled. 'Do you think life's so important as all that?'

'It's worth holding on to while we've got it,' answered Dan.

'Just run your eyes along that shelf of books,' suggested La Rue.

Dan had seen the score or so of books upon one of the shelves. He had picked them up one by one to make sure there was no weapon behind them; now he rose and began scanning them. They were books on philosophy, a subject Dan knew very little about. At La Rue's request, he handed two of them to him. La Rue opened one with his manacled hands and turned the pages until he found what he was looking for.

' "We see life, then, envisaged as a struggle,' he read, 'in which the fittest survives. Let men prate of mercy, charity, forgiveness, tenderness toward the weak — Nature knows nothing of these things. With Nature, to be strong is to be righteous, and to be cunning is to be good. That is the really divine law of life'.'

He looked up, the quizzical smile upon his face. 'What d'you make of that, Keane?' he asked.

'Is that the stuff you've been reading here?'

'That and twenty more volumes. They're translations of a great German philosopher whose name has probably never penetrated to the recesses of your intelligence, Keane. That fellow's the greatest man who ever lived. He made me what I am.'

La Rue spoke with sublime egotism; it was evident that he believed the philosopher in question should be proud of his work.

'Yes, Keane, I was a clerk in a bank

in a small western Canadian town when I came across him. He showed me the true philosophy of life. When I realized that *power* and *right* were identical, I — I was twenty thousand dollars richer within a week after I read that. I don't know whether it's worth converting you, Keane, but if once you realized that *duty* and *mercy*, and the rest of the antiquated rubbish are simply the bonds with which the *strong* hold the *weak* in subjection, you become a *man*, Keane. I'd even make you my lieutenant, because you've got the possibilities of good material, Keane.'

Dan was quite convinced now that Rue's brain was turned.

'Take pity now,' La Rue went on. 'A slave quality. The natural instinct of man is to torture, as remorselessly as the wolf tortures the rabbit. When I killed old McPherson at White's landing, I killed him slowly, Keane. As a matter of fact, he'd given me cause to dislike him. He was begging to be finished off before the end came, Keane.'

'You — damned — hound!' said Dan.

La Rue grinned. 'In yielding to the primitive instinct there, I felt a thrill of power, Keane. Do you know when I expect to feel it next? When I finish *you* off. There's a splendid finish waiting for you, Sergeant. Don't worry — it's on its way.'

Dan rose and threw another log into the stove.

Sleep was far from him when he threw himself down on his camp bed. He had never been in so eerie a situation before. He could see the flickering light playing upon La Rue's face across the room. La Rue seemed to be sleeping as peacefully as a child. And yet Dan was sure that he was plotting some fresh deviltry.

He had taken in desperate criminals several times, but never a madman, one filled with a strange and evil philosophy like La Rue. He had never been trapped with a mad criminal, with brains probably superior to his own, and the madman's wife outside, ready to steal in upon him with knife or revolver as soon as his guard was relaxed.

But either all Dan's instincts about Jehane La Rue were wrong, or else she was mad, too. He had heard that madness was contagious. Perhaps in the wilderness, fleeing with La Rue over the desolate wastes in the long darkness, Jehane La Rue had lost her mind likewise. Dan knew that in those solitudes monstrous egotisms take birth and come to dominate the mind.

There was Corporal Brody, a case well known among the police, but suppressed, as to the main details, from publication. Brody, patrolling the Arctic, had imagined himself a new Messiah, and enrolled a native army of three score who had converted the peaceful shores of the Cape Lyon district into a bloodstained bedlam until Brody was slain, and his empire suppressed — by a sergeant and two constables.

Certainly Jehane La Rue's attitude toward himself had not been consistent with sanity. Dan hoped with all his heart that she was not responsible; that the death of young Anderson could not legally be laid to her.

Still, sane or not, she was a constant peril. Dan was besieged, and unless the weather changed, or he could find the exit across the muskeg, sooner or later La Rue's threats would be justified. He had got Lafontaine, by general consent the best man-catcher in the Dominion, as he had got Anderson. And he had not been bluffing when he had announced so confidently that he would get Dan.

As he lay there, watching the firelight on La Rue's face, Dan felt that his situation was impossible. Better — if he could have known that Lafontaine was dead — to have taken Jehane in, and gone back for La Rue after. In the morning Dan meant to sound the muskeg thoroughly. In a day or two — a week at most — he must surely light upon the route across it.

He was falling asleep when of a sudden he started into intense wakefulness, conscious of a sound that he could not place somewhere on the island. He reached out for the revolver that he had taken from La Rue, and listened. As he did so, he heard the howl of a wolf near at hand, taken up by another and another.

But that was not the sound that Dan had heard. It was a continuous pattering, more like the falling of rain than anything else. But it was not rain. The stars were shining in a clear sky, and still that pattering sound went on. Dan had thought at first that it might be some trick of Jehane's, but now he knew it could not be anything of the sort, for he could hear that sound coming, apparently, from all along the side of the island.

He rose softly and went to the side of La Rue. The outlaw was sleeping, or, more probably, pretending to sleep, but Dan satisfied himself that the ropes which bound him were intact. Quietly he drew back the bolts of the door, and opened it.

There was nobody outside. The moon was low in the east, but the night was so clear, and the stars so brilliant that Dan could see the length and breadth of the little island, from the mass of limestone to the tip, and from one edge of muskeg to the other, and to the château on the elevation beyond.

Nothing seemed stirring, and at first Dan could see nothing but the trees, the muskeg, and the snow. And yet that pattering sound went on. Suddenly there sounded a scream like that of a child in mortal agony.

But he knew what it was an instant later — the death-scream of a rabbit, caught in one of Lafontaine's snares. Again a scream rang out, and then another, over by the tip of the island.

No, it was not one of the snares that had caught the creatures. It was the wolves, the pack of hunting wolves that suddenly became visible to Dan. Ranged like a file of soldiers in open order, they stood, some distance across the muskeg, the lean, long bodies, the sharp snouts and pricked ears clearly visible; and, as if they knew that the strip of muskeg acted as an insuperable bar between themselves and the island, they watched Dan, motionless and fearless.

Then of a sudden Dan saw something more, and now he knew what that pattering sound had been. Why, the snow that covered the firm ground of the island was black with rabbits, scurrying from the wolves to safety. And Dan remembered La Rue's words, 'The rabbits can cross the muskeg where the wolves can't.'

But, if the wolves could not cross, at least they had penetrated a measurable distance over the treacherous surface. Dan stared long at the place where he had seen those gray shadows, which had now vanished. The wolves had partly learned the secret; in the morning he would take up the study for himself.

He went back inside the store and closed the door. Looking at La Rue, he saw that the outlaw was now openly awake.

'Rabbits scare you, Sergeant?' he jeered. 'You ought to have seen Lafontaine that last week before Jehane caught him. I told you he had the horrors. Thought he was being mauled by rabbits every night. Between ourselves, it was the rabbits got him in the end, and not Jehane, though it wouldn't look exactly well on the police records.'

10

La Rue was apparently accustomed to captivity. He offered no objections when, after the meal, Dan trussed him up again, only asking him sarcastically whether he expected to find the road across the muskeg by dinner time.

Dan spent several hours of methodical investigation, throwing stones along the edge of the swamp at intervals of two or three feet. The work was tedious in the extreme. Here and there a stone would lie on the surface, instead of disappearing into the maw of the swamp; then Dan would set one foot carefully upon the surface, only to feel the gentle suction of the muskeg, and to see his sole slowly subsiding into the depths.

There were hard spots everywhere, but they extended for a radius of only a foot or two, as Dan's experiments with the stones proved; they were tiny islands that had hardened, with soft mire on every side of them. Not in that way was he likely to find a passage over the muck.

He returned at noon, to find La Rue deep in one of the philosophical volumes that he had placed in his hands. The captive looked up with a grin.

'Solved your problem, Keane?' he jeered.

Dan said nothing, but began the preparation of the meal — stewed rabbit, from the half dozen frozen carcasses that were hanging behind the stove.

'It's getting you the same way it got Lafontaine,' La Rue observed, closing the book with his manacled hands. 'Lafontaine was sure he couldn't be beaten by the muskeg. He was going to find a quick way out. Just a matter of a day or so, he claimed. He started throwing rocks into the swamp, at intervals of a yard or two. Your method anything along those lines, Sergeant?'

Dan, looking into the sneering face, saw absolute confidence there, the ruthlessness of power.

'Of course, the poor devil was sick with scurvy,' La Rue continued. 'After the first week it began to get on his nerves. And then the rabbits started bothering him. But that last week, before Jehane got him, he was a wreck. Screamed when I showed him a rabbit I'd caught in the wire. I guess when he looked into the muzzle of Jehane's revolver he was rather more glad to go than not.'

It was evident that La Rue was an artist in diabolism.

'But you don't go that way, Keane,' added Dan's tormentor. 'Do you know what I'm going to do to you? I'm going to make a rabbit of you.'

'In the meanwhile,' said Dan, 'the chow's ready.' He unfastened La Rue's handcuffs, and they ate.

He invited his prisoner to take some exercise in the afternoon, but La Rue declined, grinning.

'Don't want to interfere with your work, Sergeant,' he answered. 'It would spoil the afternoon for you, keeping one eye on the muskeg and the other on me. You see, you'd be watching my expression when you got 'hot' and 'cold,' trying to read how near you were to the jumping off spot. No, I'll read.'

Dan spent the rest of the afternoon in the same attempt, without better success.

That night, for some obscure reason of his own, La Rue persisted in talking about Lafontaine.

'Haven't probed for the bullet yet, have you, Keane?' he asked. 'That's important, you know. You'll find it somewhere near the other side of the head, I guess. Lafontaine's skull was thick, or it would have gone through. Once you've matched it up with the revolver, you'll have some first-rate evidence to convict. The gun you've got is the one Jehane shot him with.'

He went on talking about Lafontaine.

That night, lying awake, listening to the howling of the wolves again, and the scurrying of the rabbits, Dan could not keep his thoughts off the dead policeman.

He was not imaginative, but he could picture vividly Lafontaine's last days on the island, when, sick with scurvy, helplessly trapped, and knowing that the end was imminent, he had lain awake listening to the pattering of the rabbits and the howling of the wolves.

And the thought that Jehane La Rue had been waiting for the end, waiting to steal in upon him with the cowardly revolver shot aroused in him a loathing of the girl that transcended the loathing he felt for La Rue.

Her beauty and her seeming innocence were the masks of a devil. She had spared him only to torture him as Lafontaine had been tortured.

On the following afternoon he began to despair of finding the solution that had baffled Lafontaine. It was he, the captor, who was the prisoner, and not

La Rue. He knew that he was going the way Lafontaine had gone. And he could see, from the quizzical, sneering glances that La Rue gave him that La Rue knew.

More than once there came to him the temptation to shoot his prisoner and remove at least one of the factors in the situation. It was a temptation that would not even have entered his mind under other circumstances. Now, though he put it aside each time, each time it returned in undiminished strength.

At sunset, after the meal, he hand-cuffed and roped La Rue again and went to see Lafontaine's body.

Lafontaine lay, unchanged, upon the stretcher cot behind the fringe of stalactites, which, no longer illumined by the rays of the sun, looked like a fringe of icicles. Bending over the dead man, Dan tried to read his face.

What had been the little corporal's thoughts during those last moments when he looked into the revolver of

Jehane La Rue? Despair, at the thought that his mission had failed, or satisfaction that he had ridden upon the last patrol? Lafontaine's face was perfectly impassive; Dan could read nothing there.

Dan wondered where Jehane had trapped him. Surely she could not have obtained entrance to the store by night, with all its locks and bars!

He bent over the body and examined the wound. It was just behind the left ear, and Dan had seen it only by the merest accident when he looked upon the body before. He wondered how long La Rue would have been able to keep up the deception if he had not seen that small, carefully washed orifice under the hair. He wondered too, as he had often wondered, what had been La Rue's purpose in planning such an elaborate deception — why he had not simply taken the opportunity to get away during the period that had elapsed since Lafontaine's death.

And this seemed linked up in some way with Jehane's presence at the château. Surely they two could have got away instead of planning the impersonation which was bound to fail in the end.

Again Dan felt that there was some factor in the situation which, when explained, would throw a fresh light on everything. It was beginning to grow dark. Dan rose from beside Lafontaine He was wondering what it would be best to do, if he did succeed in thwarting the La Rue pair. He could not take in the woman as well as the man — nor the body of the dead corporal — in the absence of a sleigh. The best course would be to rush La Rue over to the Mackenzie by forced marches, and then return. He'd sweat some of that devil's philosophy out of the fellow, he thought with a grim smile. And even if he couldn't find the road, there was always the prospect of weather cold enough to freeze the muskeg. After all, Lafontaine had got across in just that way, according to La Rue's story, and La Rue would have had no particular purpose in lying on that point.

As Dan rose, his eyes fell upon the opposite wall of the rock vault. On the occasion of his former visit, with the sun throwing prismatic hues over the wall and stalactites, he had not seen it clearly. But now, in the pearly opalescence of beginning twilight, the whole interior of the cave was illumined with a diffused radiance. The wall beyond the stalactites was seamed with fissures, like the outside.

Approaching it, Dan saw that one of them was large enough to admit the body of a man. Peering through, he fancied that he could see the outlines of a second large chamber.

There would be nothing unusual in this, for every limestone formation is honey-combed with crevices and caverns, but of a sudden Dan's suspicions were awakened. For in the limestone dust that strewed the ground, he could see what looked like the faint imprints of human feet.

Of this he could not be sure. But squeezing his body through the crevice, Dan found that his belief had been correct.

He was standing in a second chamber, whose dimensions it was impossible to determine, but the air was fresh enough to indicate that it was at least as large as the outer one.

He advanced a step or two cautiously. Something soft and furry swept his face. Dan leaped back. His first impression was that he had stumbled into the den of a hibernating bear. But no sound followed and, after a moment, he advanced again, putting out his hand. Again he felt the furry object.

But this was no bear; it was the skin of some large animal. Now, as Dan's eyes began to grow accustomed to the darkness, he could see that other skins were hanging from the roof of the vault, piled up about him on shelves.

He advanced cautiously, until he

stood in the center of the chamber. There were furs on every side of him; he could see the dimensions of the room now, and though it was too dark for him to be able to distinguish one fur from another, he realized that he was in a storehouse containing a larger number of furs than ever came out of any single district of the north in a single season.

They were piled high to the roof on every side of him, packed close together in bales: some of them the rough, half-prepared skins, others soft as if they were on exhibition in the rooms of some great fur company.

And Dan knew at once what he had found. It was the store of furs stolen by La Rue and his gang from the warehouse of the murdered factor at White's Landing, and traded from the Indians for cheap hooch, or taken in the course of the outlaw's bloody raids through the Northland.

This was the cache for which the police had been seeking in vain ever since the first patrol got on La Rue's trail. And with that a good deal of the mystery was cleared up. La Rue had waited simply because to have fled would have been to leave the furs behind, whereas, by impersonating Lafontaine, had he succeeded, he could have sent Dan south in the belief that his errand had been accomplished.

The pursuit would have been called off, and La Rue would have found himself with leisure and liberty to transport the furs by degrees to points where they could enter the regular market.

Dan wondered if Lafontaine had also found the store.

He turned toward the exit, encouraged wonderfully by this discovery. All that remained now was to find the way across the muskeg. On the morrow he would renew his attempt. There was one spot where the ground seemed fairly firm.

A sound behind him startled him. He turned. Out of the darkness a form came leaping forward. Before Dan could get his revolver from his holster it was upon him.

A pistol spat.

Next instant Dan was struggling in the grip of two men, and, taken unawares, he found himself helpless. He was borne to the ground, a pile of furs tumbling down upon him.

He struggled desperately, but unavailingly. And out of the obscurity he heard the voice of Jehane La Rue, screaming, '*Don't shoot!* Don't shoot! You swore that you would not shoot!'

With a last desperate effort Dan shook off his assailants and fought himself free. As he rose to his feet a pistol butt descended upon his head, half stunning him.

He reeled — and then he saw the face of the girl peering at him out of the shadows of the interior.

At the sight of her face, framed against the darkness, his mad fury brought back his ebbing senses. He staggered toward her, shouting incoherently. He saw the terror in her eyes.

And then, abruptly as in a moving picture show, the girl's face vanished. He did not feel the second blow from behind; abruptly everything went out, and, groping through the darkness, Dan collapsed in unconsciousness at the girl's feet.

11

For a long time Dan must have been conscious of the interior of the trading store and the voices of the men without realizing it. Suddenly sight and sound were linked up within his brain. He discovered that he was lying on his camp bed again, with his eyes open, staring at the three men who were grouped about the table.

They were playing with a pack of cards in the light of the oil lamp overhead. Each of the three had a bottle of whisky and a mug beside him, and they were shouting as they slapped down the cards, and quarreling vociferously.

One of the three was La Rue; the two others were both men of enormous strength and herculean build, with bestial faces — the kind of human wolf the North turns out once in a while among her clean-limbed, simple men and women.

Dan turned his examination upon himself. He quickly discovered that he was bound fast, in the same way as that in which he had bound La Rue. Not yet fully himself, he must have uttered a groan, for La Rue glanced at him, jumped up, and flung the cards down on the table.

'*Diable*, he's awake!' he shouted in sardonic mirth. 'I thought you'd put him out for good, Lachance. His head's almost as hard as Corporal Lafontaine's!'

He advanced to Dan's side, followed by the two others. They were both mumbling, staggering drunk, but La Rue seemed sober enough to walk, to talk and gibe at his prisoner.

'Well, Sergeant, we've turned the tables, hey?' he grinned 'They don't teach you psychology in the police, do they? If they did, you might have known I was talking about Lafontaine so as to inspire you with the idea of taking another look at him. Lachance and Sirois had been waiting there all day for you to step inside. It was going to be difficult to get you in the store at night. But I laid the trap, and you walked into it.'

He grinned broadly, and Lachance and Sirois broke into roars of bestial laughter.

'I wanted to give you a longer run for your money, Sergeant,' La Rue continued. 'I wanted to trace the result of environment, and I wanted to see if you'd run true to form. Then there were the rabbits. They were beginning to get on your nerves, Sergeant. I wanted to hear you yelling for help against the rabbits in your sleep, the way Lafontaine did.

'But Jehane wanted to hurry matters up. She's got her knife into you, Sergeant. She wouldn't let you die the way Lafontaine died. We'd talked it over and fixed on what's going to happen to you. We're going to turn you into a rabbit, Sergeant. You've only got yourself to blame, you know, you walked straight into it. Give him a drink, Lachance; he'll need it bad before the night's over.'

Lachance, staggering to the table, poured out a mugful of the whisky, and brought it to Dan. He held it to his lips.

Dan turned his head aside, and Lachance dashed the contents of the mug into his face, shouting with laughter.

'You're not a good sport, Sergeant, I'm afraid,' said La Rue. 'Light a cigarette for him, Lachance.'

Lachance lit a cigarette from the butt of his old one and thrust it between Dan's lips. Dan spat it out; it dropped upon his bared throat and lay there. Dan would not wince, though the pain of the scorching flesh was agony.

La Rue, who missed nothing, bent over Dan, grinning as he peered into his face.

'Stoic, hey?' he jeered, picking up the cigarette, and pressing the lighted end into Dan's chest. 'This is only the least taste of what's coming to you, Mister Rabbit. Stoic, are you?'

With a sudden loosening of bestial fury he dashed his fists into Dan's face. Suddenly the door of the store flew open. A storm was rising, and a gust of snow-laden wind blew in. The lamp was burning low, but through the obscurity Dan could see Jehane La Rue standing in the entrance, her coat white.

Half fainting with pain, Dan vaguely was aware that his tormentors had left him to join the girl. He heard them talking, and above it all Jehane's voice raised in a horrible, shrill crescendo of manic mirth.

Then she was at his side, looking down at him, a mug of whisky in her hand. Dan would hardly have known her for the girl whom he had talked to in the tent and the château. Her face was like a devil's with insane malice, hate and triumph. And she began cursing Dan in a French *patois*, waving her arms, and shrieking like an insane woman, as she undoubtedly was.

The more she raved, the louder the three men bellowed. La Rue was drunk now like Sirois and Lachance. But when the girl unsheathed a knife and made as if to plunge it into Dan, he intervened.

'No, no, *ma belle*, we don't want to skin our rabbit before he's ready for the pot,' he shouted, catching the girl by the arm.

With a curse, Jehane drove the weapon at La Rue's throat. He caught her wrist just as the point was touching him, and gave her a backhand blow that sent her staggering, while the three rocked and howled with laughter.

Jehane rose to her feet, replacing the dagger in her belt. '*Oui, oui, mon cher*, you are right,' she answered more quietly 'Come, let us set our rabbit trap.'

At a word from La Rue, Lachance and Sirois seized Dan by the head and feet and, the rope now being unfastened, began carrying him out of the store.

What diabolical scheme La Rue had in mind he could not conjecture and he hardly cared. He was still in agony from the blows he had received on the head in the fur store; and the sight of Jehane had inspired him with a loathing of his very life. Murderess as he had known the girl to be, he had seen something in her — a fugitive glimpse of something that had inspired and almost ennobled him. It had been in the tent, that first night when he had saved her from the blizzard. And again in the château.

Ruined and desolate as the interior had been, Dan, unimaginative as he was, had seen a picture of her there, the mistress of an old seigniory. How well adapted she had seemed to be to such a part!

And now — to have seen the picture fade into that of an insane, foul-mouthed harridan was unbearable. It shook Dan's soul; it filled him with despair that made whatever torture La Rue meant to inflict upon him meaningless.

And she was still at his side as Lachance and Sirois carried him, shrieking and gibbering at him, while the gale increased every moment, blowing great clouds of snow across the island and bending the branches of the trees in a discordant symphony.

A rabbit screamed somewhere — caught in one of the wires, probably, and Dan heard La Rue's wild bellow of laughter behind him. '*Eh, mon gars*, you will be screaming like that soon,' he shouted.

Did they mean to strangle him with a wire? Dan viewed this possibility with the same lack of interest. He was very tired, and the pain in his head had become a uniform and steady throbbing, each pulsation of which was like the thrust of a knife into his brain. He had often contemplated death without undue emotion, had wondered in what guise it would come to him; but now, face to face with it, he was only conscious of a faint desire to have his whole troublesome business finished.

But suddenly Dan awoke to a new interest in the situation. They were carrying him off the island on to the muskeg. Even in that predicament his professional zeal, probably the deepest grounded of his acquirement, came to the fore. They were showing him the secret route over the swamp, and, though there was hardly the remotest chance that he would ever live to use that route, he could not help being interested.

And he peered out through the driving sleet, trying to discover the secret. They seemed to know the route thoroughly, without hesitation; nobody spoke or asked another anything about that subject. Lachance, holding Dan's legs and feet, was moving forward; Sirois following with his head and shoulders; La Rue bringing up the rear, and the madwoman stalking beside, muttering imprecations.

And of a sudden Dan understood the route, and why Lachance could lead the way without hesitation.

Lachance was stepping in a straight line from one to another of the dwarf willows, little more than shrubs that dotted the muskeg. Dan had known that the muskeg was not uniform; it consisted rather of a succession of small hummocks, with the unfathomed mire between them. And now the secret was revealed, and it was its very simplicity that had baffled Dan, as it had baffled Lafontaine.

The willows grew only where there was firm soil for their roots to take hold of. They could not grow with their roots loose in the drifting muskeg. And Lachance was stepping from willow to willow, from one firm patch to the next, until the island lay two hundred yards behind them.

It was invisible in the snow cloud that wrapped them about. The wind was mounting to a gale almost as violent as the one in which Dan had saved Jehane's life.

La Rue shouted above the wind,

'That will do! This place will do! Stand him out here!'

Next moment Dan was deposited upon the ground. With an oath, Sirois jerked him to his feet, and unfastening a length of the rope with which he was bound, began dragging him toward a small tree that emerged out of the snow.

Lachance, bellowing with laughter, grasped Dan about the body and held him against the gnarled, wind-beaten stump while Sirois adjusted the rope.

Were they going to hang him? That was Dan's first thought. But the tree was too small, too low; moreover, they were making him fast to the trunk of it, swathing him like a mummy with the coils of the rope.

His ankles were firmly knotted, thence the rope wound up his legs to his waist, which was tightly compressed by the coil; again the rope strands passed about his chest and shoulders, and, lastly, about his neck, leaving him no more than a few inches leeway.

'Leave him his hands,' bellowed La

Rue — and Jehane burst into a peal of hideous laughter. 'He'll need those. Damn this storm! I'd like to see the fun!'

Lachance and Sirois stepped back, and La Rue planted himself in front of Dan. '*Eh, mon gars,* how do you feel now, Mister Policeman?' he inquired.

Dan looked steadily at the outlaw, but did not answer.

'You know now, *hein*?' grinned La Rue. 'It was what I should have done to Lafontaine, only I did not think of it. You know now how the rabbit feels when he is in the grip of the wolf's teeth, *hein*?'

In his bestial blood fury Lafontaine had lost his veneer of cultivated speech. He had become pure hunter, the most primitive of men, rising to the heights of the utmost nobility and sacrifice, and dropping to the depths. And La Rue had plumbed those depths of his own nature often enough.

But Dan was beginning to understand. And, reckless of death though he was, the thought of *that* death sent an involuntary shudder through him, though he controlled himself well enough to keep it from La Rue's perception.

'Yes, Sergeant,' said La Rue, mimicking a child's voice, 'you are the rabbit now. Tonight the wolves are very hungry, for the rabbits stay in their burrows because of the storm. So they come creeping up, and they smell man-rabbit and they get hungrier, they begin to sniff. Then one springs and takes a bite, and the taste of human blood, it drives them mad. And then you fight with your free hands, *mon gars* — *diable*, what a battle. It is a pity no one can stay to see this night, for the wolves are timid. But in the morning we find the bones of our rabbit — *hein* Mister Policeman?'

With a final touch of brutality he kicked Dan savagely in the stomach again and again, until he hung in his ropes, doubled up with agony. But the last thing that Dan heard was the madwoman's hideous oaths and insane laughter.

12

For a long time Dan hung there, limp in his ropes, sick to death, and in almost complete unconsciousness of his surroundings.

Then slowly he began to revive. The deathly nausea passed. The throbbing pain in his head was as if somebody was beating a brazen bell, each stroke of which was accompanied by almost unbearable agony. But between the strokes Dan began to come back to himself.

The tree to which he was fastened was hardly higher than he could reach with upstretched arms, and felt little more than a sapling, but, dwarfed though it had remained, it was probably thirty years old at least, and the gnarled trunk was a mass of toughest fibre. Dan strained at it, and the pliant willow yielded, so that he could bend it this way and that; but there was no possibility of uprooting it.

And yet, hopeless as the situation seemed, Dan began to hope. Perhaps it was out of sheer despair, perhaps the reaction of a vigorous man to an impossible situation: most likely of all, that dogged resolution of the scarlet coated riders that knows no defeat short of death.

The storm was worse than the one he had encountered on the journey northward, if that had been possible. It roared over the muskeg, snapping branches from the trees, which groaned and creaked under its lashing; and on the wings of the storm came cold such as even the desolate tundra between the Bear and the Slave rarely know. It was a cold compared with which the ordinary winter cold is nothing. The thermometer outside the store registered twenty-five below that afternoon; it had dropped out of the register by midnight. It was seventy below the freezing point.

La Rue's refinement of diabolism had not gone to the extent of stripping Dan of his fur gauntlets, but as that bitter cold crept over the land Dan felt its numbing fingers gripping him, almost as if a hand had clutched him. It revived him; it called the flagging nerves and senses to one final battle against his bonds, against the human fiends and beasts of prey. Numbed, with his hands like dead weights at the ends of his arms and his feet bloodless, Dan began his last fight.

He threw his weight against the tree. He clasped his arms about it and sought to break it off at the roots till it was level with the snow, now on one side, now on the other. But always the pliant willow resumed its stance. For thirty winters it had bowed beneath the storms; it would not break for man.

Above the howling of the gale Dan could hear the drunken shouts of the men on the island. Snatches of roaring choruses came to his ears, cut off, renewed; the gang, believing themselves safe, were celebrating La Rue's liberation.

He heard it, a mocking chorus to his agony, and he fought to free himself as few men have fought before. He called on all those reserves of latent strength that lie at the summons of the will, putting forth the last ounce of them, exerting every muscle in the battle. And in the end he was beaten.

He acknowledged himself beaten. He had done all that man could do, and he had neither broken the tree nor loosened his bonds. The frozen rope was a chain of ice, inflexible as steel, and, like steel, it had bitten deep gashes in his legs and arms.

Then through the gale Dan heard the distant howling of the wolf pack. And over the snow the patter of the rabbits began. Invisible, lithe little forms were darting past on either side of him. One hurled itself in panic against him, rebounding like a stone. The patter was continuous as the rain, and louder across the muskeg sounded the howls of the hunting pack.

Then a gaunt form broke through the willows within a few yards of Dan, leaped almost to his feet, and recoiled, snarling.

Dan, who had ceased to struggle, slumped forward in his ropes, drawing in great gulps of air. He was at the end of his resources, and almost incapable of movement.

He had heard varying stories as to the ferocity of timber wolves. Some said that when sufficiently famished, they would not hesitate to attack man; others that they never attacked a human being. He knew that it is the degree of hunger that counts; wolves, when their stomachs have been empty long enough, will attack anything — a party of men, if they are emboldened by the presence of the pack.

Dan peered out through the driving snow, but he could see only two or three feet in front of him — the outlines of the little willows on the muskeg, merging into the darkness. Yet, as he strained his eyes, he seemed to see shadows moving in that darkness — lean, stealthy forms, beginning to circle him, but so faint that he could not he sure whether he actually saw anything.

Minutes passed. Through the gale he could still hear the drunken yells of the three outlaws on the island. He was slowly gathering fresh strength for the fight which he knew to be inevitable — the last fight. He would go down fighting. It should be mercifully short, once the attack began.

And it came as Dan had anticipated that it would come. Without a sound, without the slightest warning, a shape launched itself out of the shadows, straight toward Dan's throat.

It overleaped him and missed, and with that the fury of the primal man was unleashed in Dan. He had thought he would go down in a grim, silent struggle; instead, a cry of which he was not conscious broke from his throat, and stark against the tree, he braced himself for battle.

*   *   *

The hell's scum on the island heard that cry above the howl of the wind. A roar of mirth came from La Rue; he staggered up from the table at which he and the other two were seated.

'They've got him!' he shrieked. 'Did you hear that, Sirois? They're tearing at him! Listen, listen! Rabbit pie out on the muskeg! God, I'd give ten years of my life to see it! I'm going!'

'Don't be a fool, Alphonse! They'll get you, too,' mumbled Sirois, leaning, glassy-eyed, across the table. Lachance was sprawling with his head among the cards, clutching the money that he had won.

La Rue went to the door and opened it. He fell back as a cloud of snow came bursting in, and slammed it again.

'God, what a night! I guess they've got him by this time,' he muttered.

'Hey, Lachance! Wake up!' He shook the half-conscious man until he sat up, scowling and muttering. 'The night ain't over yet. Shuffle the deck. I'm going to win back what you won — damn you, d'you hear me?'

★　★　★

As the wolf leaped again, Dan's fist caught it full in the slavering jaws. The impact of the beast, this time against Dan's breast, bent the tree almost to the ground, and carried Dan with it, but the wolf, momentarily dazed by the blow, rolled undermost. It retreated, snarling. Dan, jerked back upon his feet by the rebounding of the willow, awaited the onset of the pack. Two forms broke through the snow spume. Before Dan had quite understood what was happening, one of them was slashing at the ropes that bound him.

They parted, and then, numbed and incredulous, Dan found himself face to face with the girl and the Indian, Louis.

It was too incredible to be true. For a moment Dan lost touch altogether with reality; then the thought came to him that the girl had been playing a part in the store, in order to help him. But there was no time for speculation. Louis was thrusting a long knife into his hands.

'Quick, Monsieur, this way!' he gasped. 'Don't touch your skin to the blade, or you will lose it!'

He turned to run, tugging at the girl's arm, and as Dan stumbled in their wake another of the shadows leaped, and then another and another. In another moment the three were beset by the maddened pack. Dan thrust and hacked, dealing furious slashes, as did the Indian. They tumbled in a bloody welter on the snow. Dan felt teeth meet in his shoulder through his mackinaw, and, maddened with the pain, he drove the knife upward clear through the furry throat, pulled it free, and rose from beneath the carcass of the dying beast.

Louis was struggling with two more of the wolves. Dan saw the knife thrust of the Indian rip through the hide along the whole length of the belly. The second beast leaped for the Indian's throat. Before the jaws could close, Dan had struck home.

They were free. Dan and the Indian had the girl by either arm, supporting her. They ran three or four paces, turned to face the menacing pack, and ran on again. The dying wolves were already being torn asunder, but others of the pack were following the fugitives, leaping short and cowering back into the night, but always following. It was a fight against shadows for now they could see nothing, and again a form would leap and vanish. It was the way the wolves tired out the caribou and separated the fawns from the herd. But suddenly the girl uttered a scream and, swinging around, Dan saw three shadows crouching, as if to leap upon their other side.

He forestalled them, running forward, shouting. The shadows vanished but at the same moment there rang out a piercing cry from Louis, and then a scream of agony.

Dan ran to his side — too late. The old man had slipped on the snow and half the pack was snarling over his remains. Before Dan reached his side the Indian had been rent literally limb from limb.

His rush sent the wolves scurrying back and sick with horror, Dan bent over what had been Louis. But again the girl screamed, almost at his side, and as Dan turned a huge gray shape shot past him, the blow of the glancing body sending the girl staggering into Dan's arms. Had either fallen, it would have been the end. But Dan kept his feet, and as he backed away, the pack again hurled themselves upon the Indian's body, and the hideous howl of triumph rose into the air.

Momentarily the two were left alone, for the whole pack was snarling over the remains, and Dan, holding the girl, backed toward the fringe of brush which, looming up in the darkness, told him that they had crossed the muskeg and were almost upon the firm ground at the edge of the muskeg lake. He turned and ran with her, turned again, peering into the shadows and glaring around him, and turned and ran once more. Now they were rounding the lake's edge, and the girl went limp in Dan's hold.

'We're safe!' she gasped. 'They — never come — this side of the lake.'

And she collapsed, a dead weight in his arms.

Dan lifted her — his own arms were numb almost to the shoulder, and carried her up the slope toward the old château. From time to time he halted and looked back, but they were no longer being followed. Beyond the lake Dan could hear the snarling of the pack as they fought over their prey; it ceased, and then came another long-drawn howl of triumph, first from one throat and then from another, and perhaps the most terrible of all the sounds made by the beasts that kill.

Holding the girl close to him, Dan staggered on. He was on the plateau now, and in front of him, through the trees, loomed up the outlines of the château. It was completely dark. Dan felt as if his strength would just suffice him to the door. If it were locked, he would be finished.

But it swung open to his push, and he staggered in, clasping the girl's unconscious body still more closely. He staggered in in a furious gust of wind and snow, and then the warmth of the stove, still burning in the big hall, came to him like the sun out of heaven.

Dan stumbled down the long room. He remembered that there was a lounge in the room beyond, on the right of the door. A second stove was burning in the further room, its light, reflected through the chinks, faintly illumining it. Dan found the lounge and laid the girl down on it; then he toppled over on the floor at her feet, and knew nothing more.

13

The agony of the returning circulation roused him. Every inch of his body ached with a thousand tortures. Dan groaned, stirred, opened his eyes, and looked about him, without knowing where he was. For the moment his memory carried him forward only to the time when he had been upon the island, with La Rue his prisoner.

Then a clock somewhere chimed the hour of four in soft, melodious strokes, and with that his senses became coordinated, and the pain in his hands and feet, which had been impersonal, attached itself more deeply to his consciousness.

Dan groaned again. Then he felt his hands being rubbed briskly, and realized that he was lying upon the lounge in the château, and that the girl was kneeling beside him, working over him in the light of a single candle.

As consciousness revived, the pain increased. He felt racked in every sinew and muscle of his body. The pain of the returning blood flow was almost unendurable, but in addition to that his head was throbbing as if it was about to split, and there was a burning numbness in his left shoulder, which felt as if it was bandaged.

Dan's eyes, wandering downward, fell upon his clothes. His mackinaw had been removed, and his shirt was stiff with dried blood. Dan remembered.

He remembered, but he was too weak to feel much horror at that remembrance, though again he saw the snarling jaws about him, and Louis, rent and dismembered almost in an instant. He watched the girl through half closed eyelids as she tended him. How strong and capable her face looked as she worked, massaging his wrists and ankles alternately with steady, untiring strokes. Was that the madwoman who had screamed blasphemies at him in the store on the island?

Once more life and death had been tossed to and fro between them, and again he owed his life to her, to La Rue's wife, the murderess, who must hang upon a gibbet in some prison yard!

Suddenly the girl, as if conscious that she was being watched, shot a swift glance upward, and met Dan's eyes. She withdrew her hands.

'Now you will be all right, Sergeant Keane,' she said, looking at him with an inscrutable expression in her eyes.

'How long have you been working over me?' asked Dan.

'About two hours. It was exhaustion, I think, more than the cold.'

Two hours, after her own exposure, after the horrors of the night! Dan did not know what to say. But now he began to be aware that he had not been altogether unconscious after all. Even while he lay in a torpor he had somehow been aware of the passage of time, of the girl's lifting him upon the couch and tending him, and of a screaming somewhere — over on the island — shrill, prolonged and horrible.

'I think you will be able to walk after a little. I bandaged your shoulder. There was only a small flesh wound there.' She shuddered, and caught at the frame of the couch, as if about to faint. For an instant her body went limp and her eyes closed; then she recovered herself. 'Sergeant Keane, I have something to say to you,' she went on with swift eagerness. 'I am going to offer to surrender myself to you. I will pledge you my word of honor to make no attempt to escape if you will accept it. Place me on parole, so that I can look after you until you are stronger. In your present state you are in no condition to think of arresting my — my husband. Besides, I should never again take you across the muskeg. Place me on parole, then.'

Dan continued to watch her. This

was not the language of a vicious murderess; the girl's manner, her looks, her whole demeanor were inconsistent with those of the woman who had screamed at him so venomously upon the island — who had trapped him in the fur cache.

'You can't take us both in at the same time,' the girl went on, twisting and untwisting her fingers nervously. 'So take me, and leave my husband. I don't want my freedom now, or my life either. I want to end — everything.'

Still Dan said nothing, and she went on with still more feverish eagerness.

'We are safe here until it grows light. That gives us four hours' start. They suppose that you — died — out on the muskeg. In four hours we can throw them off our trail completely. I want to take you to a place I know of. It is a little cabin, hidden in a belt of forest a few miles away. Poor Louis built it for me secretly a year or two ago, so that if ever I — found that my life had grown intolerable — I could go there and be free.'

She was speaking now with desperate eagerness. 'I want you to let me take you there until you have recovered,' she went on. 'You see, it is impossible for you to find the way across the muskeg, you are unarmed, and as soon as the storm ceases and it grows light they will discover what has happened, and then they will come here and murder you. You are no match for the three of them, weak and unarmed. Come with me and I will hide you, and then, when you are well, you shall take me back to the police post with my own sleigh and the dogs. They are at Louis' cabin, a quarter of a mile away. Come with me!'

The words flowed from her lips with certain incoherence; it was the babbling of a soul at its last extremity. And as he watched her a light began to break for him.

'You wish to surrender yourself, Madame La Rue?' he asked. 'You offer your free surrender, provided I take you in first, and then return for your husband?'

'Yes, yes,' she panted. 'It was I killed Corporal Anderson. I will write out a complete confession. You might as as well take me first, since you cannot take us both together.'

Dan sat up with an effort. He was feeling better now, stronger, though every nerve was a little center of individual pain.

'I am not deceived any longer,' he said quietly. 'You are not Jehane La Rue. You are not the woman who tried to kill me in my tent, nor are you the woman who trapped me in the fur cache. Who are you?'

'I don't know what you mean!' cried the girl wildly. 'Who else could I be but Jehane La Rue? Didn't I try to kill you — *twice*, and then repent, because I — couldn't bring myself to — ?'

'No,' answered Dan. 'No, you couldn't act well enough for that. And so I think it would be best to tell me the truth, Mademoiselle Desmoulins!'

She started back, staring at him in panic, one hand clutched to her breast. 'You — know my name — '

'Louis called you Mademoiselle Camille. Your surname I got from La Rue, the man you quite impossibly tried to pretend was your husband. I knew that couldn't be true. Come, Mademoiselle, it is useless to try to deceive me any longer. You are not Jehane La Rue. In consequence, you have nothing to gain by pretending to be that person any longer. I know, of course, that she is your sister. The resemblance is too close for her to be anything else. Tell me the truth!'

For a moment or two the girl continued looking at Dan, clasping and unclasping her hands with agitated movements. Then she surrendered.

'I'll tell you the truth, then,' she answered. 'There's nothing else to do.'

'Tell me all,' said Dan. 'I think that will be the best.'

'I'll tell you everything as quickly as I can. Well, my father was Arture

Desmoulins. He was in the fur trade. He had built up a business rivaling that of the big companies, by just dealings. He spent half the year up here, and the rest in Montreal, where we had our home as children.

'Mother was dead, and we were at a school half the year, but we always looked forward to my father's return. We worshipped him, Jehane and I.

'One day — I was a child then, and did not understand what it all meant — my father told us that he was going into the north and would never come back. Afterward I knew what had happened. His business had been destroyed by unscrupulous rivals; there was a warrant for his arrest on the charge of extensive frauds, though I knew that he was innocent, for he was the soul of honor. But he faced a term of years in prison, and he knew it would mean his death, and he feared for our future. We were only children, and everything was gone. All our friends deserted us, and a warrant had already been issued for his arrest.

'He was the subject of universal execration, for the shares of the company that he had formed had gone down to nothing, and hundreds of poor people who had invested their money in it because they believed in him had lost everything. And that was the one thing he could not bear.

'He knew this district, and he knew that at certain seasons certain fur-bearing animals fled here from the wolves and other beasts that preyed on them. He believed that he could grow rich in a few years, and repay everything he owed. So he built this château, and the cabin on the island, which was not an island then. Later an arm of the muskeg river flowed around it on this side and cut it off.

'Here I grew up. My father taught me, and I taught Jehane, my little sister. The venture prospered, and little by little the furs that my father sent out became known for their richness. Little by little all those who had trusted my father were repaid with interest, and the warrant for his arrest was withdrawn. Before he died, we owed nothing!'

She spoke proudly, with flashing eyes, and Dan forgot his own pain in wondering at her pride and courage.

'And always the talk was of the day when we should return. But we had all come to look upon this as our home. Only little Jehane, who had been too young to remember very much of Montreal, was restless and dissatisfied.

'Then came the day when Louis brought my father home. He had carried him ten miles on his back. My father had been crushed by a falling tree while following his trap line. His spine was broken, and he had lain for two days and nights in the bitter cold. Only his intense vitality had saved him.

'He might have lived, a cripple, but it was the cold that killed him. The frozen limbs gangrened, and there was no hope of saving him. Before he died he called me to his side and made me swear that I would always watch over little Jehane.

'He was in great distress about her, for he knew what was in her mind, and he was afraid for her. I told him that I would give my life for her, if necessary. And I meant to fulfill that promise, if ever the time came.'

She seemed to have forgotten Dan's presence; the confession had become a monologue, the outpouring of the pent-up emotions of years.

'It came after Alphonse La Rue came to the château, seeking refuge one stormy night. He was a newcomer in the district, and we had never seen him before, but he was almost the first white man Jehane had ever seen since she was a child, except an occasional missionary or trader.

'I read everything — Jehane's infatuation, and Alphonse La Rue's cold, deliberate calculations. After he had gone, saying that he would be back before the summer, I told Jehane that we would go back to Montreal. We had a little money put by, enough to have kept us for a year or two. And always Jehane had been urging me and always I had begged her to wait a little longer, for Louis was working for us, and slowly the money was accumulating.

'But now she refused. She had changed. Alphonse La Rue had possessed her very soul, as he had done ever since. I will be as quick as I can, Monsieur,' the girl went on, as if becoming conscious of Dan again. 'Long before the summer he was back, and he stayed, and went, and stayed. This part of the story is our own inviolable secret, Jehane's and mine.

'But I succeeded in forcing him to marry her at the mission on the Great Slave. They came back here. He stepped into my father's shoes. Little by little I discovered what kind of a man he was — worse than I had feared. Then he brought his men here, outlaws who had joined him, and this became their headquarters.

'Often I begged Jehane to come with

me and let us escape together, and she would agree, for she was desperately unhappy, but as soon as La Rue returned she fell into his power again.

'After her child was born dead, it seemed as if a devil had taken possession of her. And then — I cannot tell you, but — she committed a crime that put her outside the pale of the law. But it was he — Alphonse La Rue, who had played upon her weak nature until he had made her morally his slave.

'The rest is quickly told. They were hunted from place to place, and at last came back here for refuge. I knew my sister's hands were stained with blood. I knew that Corporal Lafontaine was on his way to arrest Alphonse and that those two had laid their plans to kill him. They suspected my intentions, and I was kept a prisoner till — it was done.

'I had managed to get Lafontaine's last message to headquarters sent out through Louis, but I could get no warning to Lafontaine himself, and Louis had no opportunity of speaking to him. Then, when it became known that you were coming, I went down to meet you. When I couldn't turn you from your purpose, and I discovered that you had a warrant for Jehane's arrest, I — I called in Sirois and Lachance. They had been waiting near, to help remove the furs as soon as you were dead. They swore, and Alphonse swore that you should not be hurt. But they lied to me. Then I thought that perhaps I might take my sister's place, and die for her, in memory of my dead father, and my promise to him — '

14

The tears came in a relieving flood, and Dan, sitting up on the couch, watched the girl, knowing that in all probability they had saved her reason. The clock chimed five. The candle was guttering low. Outside the gale was still raging, though Dan thought that its violence was abating. Whatever he did, he would have to do it quickly.

In a minute or two Camille had recovered her self-possession. She turned to Dan. 'And now you know all, Monsieur,' she said. 'I would have died for her, but, since it was of no use, I must put myself in your hands. I cannot go on any longer, and I know now that I was wrong in trying to save him from the consequences of his crimes. After last night — it is better that he should die.'

'Where is Jehane?' asked Dan.

Camille looked at him for a moment with the old suspicion. 'You are going to take her, then? A madwoman whom the law cannot hang? You have seen enough of her to know that her brain is gone. It went after the birth of her child. Without him, she is powerless. Monsieur, I beg of you, let me take you to that place I told you of, till you are recovered. Then — God help us all — you must do as you will.'

'Where is Jehane?' asked Dan again.

Camille seemed to collapse under the insistent question. Dan saw that she had not yet abandoned hope of saving her sister.

'Ah, you are *terrible*, you *policemen*! Like *machines*, merciless! *Take the man* — *in God's name take the man*, not the woman, who is mad — '

'You *must* tell me where Jehane is,' said Dan again. 'I do not know what I shall do. First, where is she?'

'*She is here, then!*' Camille cried.

'Here?' Dan glanced about him quickly. For a moment he had thought that Jehane was in the room with them.

'She is in the château — down below. Louis and I locked her in the room where my father stored his furs after the muskeg cut us off from the island. It is cold there, but she has rugs and blankets, and what could I do? She fought — *ah, mon Dieu*, she is mad, I tell you! She came to me with a revolver, telling me that you had been thrown to the wolves, threatening me, hating me, this sister for whom I would have given my life.'

'I must see her.'

'Monsieur Keane, *think, think first*, I implore you! They will find her and release her in the morning. She will suffer, but not as she would have made you suffer. Monsieur, come with me. There is no time to be lost — '

But Dan was already on his feet. He found that he could stand, though the frostbites were agonizing, and the throbbing in his head and shoulder seemed hardly to have decreased.

He did not yet know what course he

meant to pursue, but it was in his mind to accept Camille's proposal, since he could not hope to cope with La Rue and his men till he grew stronger. In the meantime, however, he would take Jehane with them.

He said nothing of this; he was not sure of himself. He motioned to the girl to pick up the candle and lead the way. After a moment of what seemed to indicate defiance, Camille obeyed, with a helpless shrug of her shoulders, and, picking up the guttering light, preceded Dan through the large room into another one behind it.

This seemed to have been a kitchen, but now it was quite empty, so far as Dan could see by the flickering light. There was a hole in the roof at the farther end, and the floor lay three inches deep with snow there. Outside the wind was still howling; the bitter cold was in striking contrast with the warmth of the stove-heated room in which they had been.

Holding the candle high, Camille

opened a door communicating with a passage, at the end of which appeared a flight of wooden steps. The wind, whistling through chinks in the log walls which were stuffed with moss, almost blew out the light. Camille, shielding it with her hand, began to descend the steps. Halfway down, she paused and turned.

'She is in here, Monsieur, fastened tightly,' she said, pointing to the door at the bottom.

Dan hobbled down the stairs and preceded the girl, taking the candle from her hand. The heavy door at the bottom of the flight was secured with an iron bar, probably to protect the furs that had once been stored in the vault against human or animal marauders. Dan raised it. The cold stung his frostbitten hands.

He pushed it back, 'Madame La Rue!' he called.

But no answer came, and Camille, now at his side, looked at him in piteous entreaty.

'Take care, Monsieur! If she has managed to free herself — though I do not see how she could have done so — she is dangerous. She — '

She was looking in at Dan's side. The vault was a large one, damp and chill. At intervals wooden posts supported the roof, which was the floor of one of the rooms above. Camille took the candle from Dan and moved it slowly, so that its light illuminated different parts of the interior. Suddenly she uttered a cry, and lowered the candle slightly, pointing to one of the posts nearby.

At the foot of it a rope lay in a heap, showing where the prisoner had freed herself, either by sleight of hand or by the strength of madness. And beyond it, at the further end of the vault, was an open door, showing where she had made her exit.

A gust of wind came through, making the expiring candle flicker brightly.

Camille caught Dan by the arm. 'Monsieur Keane, she must have freed herself. She has gone to the muskeg. Whether or not she knows that you were in the house, she will bring *them* back to wreak their vengeance on me for having bound her. They have long suspected that I wished to help you. We must start at once. We — '

A violent gust of wind blew out the candle. Dan half turned. Suddenly a scream broke from Camille's lips. With a violent movement she flung herself in front of Dan. She screamed again, and sank in a heap at the bottom of the stairs.

Simultaneously the shriek of the madwoman rang echoing through the thick and impenetrable darkness of the vault, a shriek of mockery that resounded from wall to wall as if a score of fiends had taken up the chorus.

Dan did not know what had happened. He was almost unnerved by that hideous ribald laughter, but he obeyed the impulse that came immediately into his mind.

He leaped from Camille's side and

pulled the door to, shutting the madwoman within. No matter if there was an exit at the other end, he was glad to have that door between them. He replaced the bar, picked Camille up in his arms, and made his way up the stairs, feeling his passage through the empty kitchen and back into the boudoir where he laid her down on the couch.

He called to her, but she seemed in a dead faint, and helplessly in the dark Dan began searching for a light.

Fortunately he had not far to search. Upon the little table beside the lounge he found a box of matches. Striking one, he saw another candle standing at his hand and in another moment had it alight and had turned to Camille again.

She lay upon the lounge, her face waxen-white, and to Dan's horror he saw blood running down her dress from a cut at the back of the shoulder.

He tore apart the woven mackinaw, and the material beneath, and saw that the blood was welling thickly from a gaping wound inflicted by the mad-woman's knife. How deep it was there was no means of determining, but in the light of the candle Camille's lips looked blue and she was gasping for breath.

Still, there was no blood upon her lips and that gave Dan hope that the lung had not been pierced. But he knew that it was Camille's instinctive leap in front of him that had saved his own life. That slash of the knife of Jehane La Rue had been meant for him. She had freed herself from the ropes with which she was bound, and cunningly awaited them; perhaps she had stolen in upon them and listened to Camille's confession — perhaps she was even now stealing in on them again.

Dan reached out his foot and slammed the door between the boudoir and the hall. That shut off any unheralded approach save from the rear, and Jehane would have to cross the lighted room to reach him. He began with clumsy first-aid methods to try to stop the flow of blood.

At first it seemed as if it would never cease, as if the girl's life was ebbing away. Then slowly Dan began to get the upper hand. He bound the wound tightly with strips of cloth that he pulled from the rent in Camille's mackinaw, soft linen stuff he hated to despoil. And in the end she was lying back on the lounge, and the flow seemed to have been checked.

The little clock chimed half-past the hour of six, but there was still an hour and a half till dawn. The wind was going down; only fitfully did it shake the house or whistle about the eaves. The cold was in the room. Dan thrust on the last of the birch logs that were piled beside the stove. They would last two hours. And in the next two hours he meant to force the matter to its final issue.

There was a vessel of water in the kitchen, and Dan filled a cup that he found with the aid of a candle, and went back to the girl's side. He kneeled by her, looking into her face. It was so white, her lips so bloodless she seemed hardly to breathe! And yet Dan was glad of the happenings of that night, taken all in all, for they had given him back the faith that he had lost. They had showed him loyalty and self-sacrifice of which he had not believed any woman capable. And there, beside Camille, Dan registered a vow that he would acquit himself of the task before him, and save her life as well.

Her lips moved, and he heard her whisper his name. He tried to pour a little of the water between them, knowing the thirst that follows so great a loss of blood, but barely succeeded. He looked at the bandage, and found that the flow had not restarted. And, standing beside the girl, Dan fought the hardest and bitterest fight of his whole life.

He was going *back*, going back to the muskeg, to try to find his way across the willows. And he was going back unarmed, to face three desperate men, trusting to surprise and to such weapon as he might succeed in finding — a bough, an iron bar, whatever came to his hand. He was going back, frostbitten, wearier than he had thought it possible for a man to be, with a splitting head and a shoulder maimed by the teeth of a wolf. He was going back, in obedience to the inexorable law of the Force he served and worshiped.

He was going back, with hardly the smallest hope that he would return. If he escaped the wolves, there was the muskeg. If he escaped the muskeg, there were the three desperadoes. There was the madwoman, wandering from house to camp, and filled with a blind hate that might vent itself on Camille while he was away.

He was going on his last mission, and, if he failed to return, Camille would die.

He knew that, and because the law of the Police requires that everything be subordinated to her service, he did not flinch from the issue.

He looked once more at the unconscious girl. She was lying back on the lounge, white and still. And he felt the strength of the sacrifice flow into his soul and fill it.

Turning, Dan put out the candle, and, with firm steps, made his way through the boudoir, through the hall, and to the door of the château.

Dan pushed to the front door and stepped out into the storm. The wind was still blowing hard, but the snow had almost ceased, and the cold was still increasing. Dan had never known such cold in all his experience of the North. It acted as a tonic, but he knew that he must find the path across the muskeg quickly, or he would perish in the snow.

Suddenly, as he left the château, the screams of Jehane La Rue rang out again. Three times that piercing shriek came over the marsh, and then followed silence.

Dan shuffled over the snow. He had no snowshoes, but the hard surface was like a cinder-track. He skirted the muskeg lake until he reached the fringe of trees from which a diagonal route ran to the island.

The first faint streaks of dawn showed against the dun clouds in the east. Dan must have remained much longer at Camille's side than he had realized. He could now see the willows dotting the muskeg, and cautiously began to feel his way to the nearest clump.

It was not until he had passed several clumps that the truth broke up on him. The entire surface of the muskeg was frozen by the bitter cold!

Dan moved tentatively aside from the willows. Yes, it was true; the muskeg had grown firm in a single night; but for his surprise in the fur cache he could have been on his way with La Rue within a few hours.

Dan strode forward resolutely, peering through the faint, opalescent beginnings of twilight to discern the mass of limestone at the head of the

189

island. Suddenly a wolf howled close at hand, and Dan saw the lean shape skulking into the trees.

He went on. Now he could distinguish the blurred outlines of the limestone; and now he stood upon the island. Now, through the trees, he saw the store gradually detach itself from the flat obscurity of the darkness and take form.

Dan moved forward slowly. He was making his plans. Where was Jehane La Rue? Had she warned the crew that he had escaped them, and was still alive? Had he been tracked, were the plans for his final taking off already matured?

His only chance lay in a sudden rush. If he could overcome any one of the three, and get possession of his gun, he would have the barest fighting chance for success. He thought of Camille in the château, lying unconscious and at death's door. That thought steadied him, gave him a new draft upon whatever reserves of strength remained to him.

He was nearing the store. Dawn was breaking fast; already he must be visible to anyone watching from within. And nowhere was there shelter. He must go forward openly —

He was behind the angle of the building and still everything remained still. The door was open! In the gathering light Dan could see that it swung right back against the exterior of the building. He crept forward foot by foot, mentally computing the instant for the rush.

Now he was behind the door. He listened. No sound came from within. And Dan had a growing feeling that the ambuscade he had imagined did not exist. He could feel that there was no one waiting on the other side of the door.

He leaped. With three bounds he was within the store.

The echo of his feet upon the yielding boards was the only sound that came to his ears. And, peering through the twilight of the interior, Dan saw that the store was empty!

The table was upset, the chairs were lying on their sides, there was broken glass everywhere, and — so bitter was the cold — there were pools of frozen whisky on the floor.

Dan glared about him. There must have been a struggle there. It looked as if the three men had fallen to blows.

The whisky had been spilled in drops running from the table to the door. But those drops were not all whisky. Dan could distinguish more plainly now. They were blood — so red was the pool beside the table.

Murder had been done that night, but who had been murdered by whom it was impossible as yet to know.

Dan went to the door. He saw now that the snow was trampled all about the building, and there were bloodstains everywhere. But from the building toward the muskeg there ran a broad trail in the snow, as if some heavy body had been dragged over its surface in the direction of the muskeg. And still that trail of blood ran on and on.

Straight over the muskeg Dan traced it in the dawning day, until it came to an end among the willows. And there Dan found all that remained of Sirois and Lachance.

With that, light broke in upon him. The wolves had crossed the muskeg, and, maddened by hunger, had seized the two outlaws while they lay drunk and senseless within the store.

But there was no sign of La Rue's body, and, following the trail back to the store, Dan now perceived that another one led toward the cave.

Straight through the fissure it ran, and outside the snow bore the imprints of the pads of wolves. Here they had leaped at the fissure and fallen back again, here they had milled, seeking the entrance, yet lacking just that modicum of intelligence that would have enabled them to squeeze through one by one.

Dan halted outside. 'La Rue!' he called. 'Give up! I've got you!'

No answer came, and, without

hesitation, Dan squeezed through. He saw the fringe of stalactites, and the body of Lafontaine behind it; he looked about him but could see nothing more.

But a faint crooning sound came from within the fur cache behind, and Dan, after calling again, and receiving no reply, stepped through.

It was still almost dark within, but there was just light enough for him to distinguish the outlines of the two figures on the ground.

One was Jehane La Rue. She crouched, La Rue's body in her arms, and was crooning, as one croons to a child.

Dan touched her on the shoulder and spoke to her; she continued crooning, as if completely oblivious of his presence.

Dan kneeled down and looked at La Rue. The outlaw had just died, for the body was not yet cold. He was horribly mangled. In his mind Dan reconstructed the last dreadful scene — the rush of the wolves, the seizure of

Lachance and Sirois. La Rue's desperate fight for life as he made for the cave. And those shrieks of Jehane's had signaled her discovery of him.

He drew the dead man out of Jehane's arms. 'Come!' he said to the girl. 'There is no use in staying here any longer.'

She did not hear him, but she rose to her feet when he pulled at her arm, and let him lead her back to the château.

Those weeks that followed were never much more than a dream to Dan. At first they were a dream of fear and anguish, when he fought death, hour by hour, for the possession of Camille.

There were hours of despair when life seemed slowly ebbing; but there were hours of intense happiness when he began to hope that the fight was won.

Dan had never fought that kind of a fight before, for he himself was for days in the grip of the fever devil, as the result of the wolf-bite. There were days when he roused himself from his delirium to attend to Camille, to get food for her and the woman whose mind had gone forever, and left her mentally like a year-old child. Somehow Dan won through.

So that at last there came the day when Camille and he stood at the door of the château together, the sleigh and harnessed dogs beside them, and Jehane seated on the sleigh, staring into vacancy.

Lafontaine's body, with the remains of Louis and La Rue, had been committed to the muskeg till that day when it will give up its secrets.

Camille looked at Jehane. 'I feel — somehow — it is the best that could have happened,' she said, 'short of death. I feel in a way that I have won my little sister back again. Sometimes I think she knows me, and I am sure the past, with its sins and sufferings, has gone from her mind forever.'

Dan heard her only vaguely. He was thinking of their journey south together to the mission on the Great Slave, where they were to be married.

And in the air were the first scents of spring.

Postponed Verdict

Killbee had grown from a logging camp to a lumber center to a sizable small town in twenty years. It was becoming known to sportsmen, who came every season to hunt mountain sheep. There were grizzlies, too, if you went far enough into the mountains: back into the recesses of the second growth of Douglas fir that had sprung up and clear up to the glacier line, where the slow-moving ice from Mount Crow, always snowbound, dissolved into a torrent of foaming water.

James Brennan had started with a tiny sawmill a quarter century before. Luck, bluff, and hard, two-fisted dealing had made him president of the big Killbee Lumber Company. He had his winter home in Los Angeles, and left his affairs in charge of his manager, Flaherty, who was as tough as Brennan had been in his prime. He drove his men hard, and kept their wages down to the lowest point he dared. There was no other industry in the town. The men had struck once, and their wives and kids had starved. The strike was broken.

There was just one period of the year when Brennan stayed three weeks or so at Killbee. That was in the summer, after the logging season was over, in the slack of the year, when men loafed about their homes, and their wives tried to stretch their savings until the time when work would start again. Brennan had come back every year for the big-game hunting. Each year for five-and-twenty years he'd gone out after elk, sheep, and black-tail deer.

Brennan was a big man now. Pictures of his wife and daughter at fashionable gatherings in Los Angeles occasionally reached Killbee town in the California newspapers. It was twenty years since he had lost his first wife, high up on Mount Crow. She had been a local girl. Maybe it was just as well. She wasn't the social kind that the second Mrs. Brennan seemed to be.

Brennan was high-handed on those visits to the hunting-lodge he had built. Killbee town hated him silently. About as much as his man Flaherty. There wasn't much to choose between them, except that Flaherty was more of a rough-neck, and Brennan had learned diplomacy.

And Brennan hadn't the smallest idea that through all those twenty years that had passed, since he lost his first wife, Mabel, disaster had been slowly and inevitably creeping up on him, and that it could be measured in two dimensions — by time, and by inches.

Jim Greer, the sheriff, had got into office because it hadn't seemed worth Flaherty's while to trouble to set up a sheriff of his own. As for Brennan, of course he left everything to his manager. The old sheriff, who had died, had been useful in getting the lumber-jacks out of trouble, and it paid Flaherty to stand by his men. At

Christmas, a month after Jim's election, Flaherty sent him a box of cigars and a case of bourbon.

The bourbon said, in effect, 'We're all good fellows. No prohibition stuff up here.'

When Jim returned the gift, with a polite note explaining that he couldn't accept it, Flaherty smelled a rat. That rodent became more odoriferous a week or two later, when one of Flaherty's toughs got drunk and beat up old Cronin, whose daughter Mabel had been Brennan's first wife, twenty years before. Flaherty came to the jail in person. 'You can't lock up my man,' he said. 'I need him for the logging.'

Jim shrugged his shoulders. 'He's here,' he said.

'What do you think you're going to do with him?' sneered Flaherty.

'Turn him over to the county prosecutor. This is a case of violent assault and battery.'

Flaherty tried persuasiveness. 'You're

new at the law game, Mr. Greer,' he said. 'You don't seem to realize that the Lumber Company is the law up here. I'll discipline the man. You turn him loose.'

When Jim just grinned, the big man roared, and declaimed: 'I'll have you busted for this! I'll show you who's boss around these parts! You can't come into Killbee and act like as if you owned the town.'

Jim said: 'They told me Killbee was a tough place, on account of some of your crowd, Mr. Flaherty. That's why they did not elect a local man. Go and sit on a log.'

Flaherty cooled off, and departed. He knew when he was up against the real thing. He went off, after giving Jim a sardonic warning.

Two state policemen came for the prisoner. Flaherty's man was taken away, and got six months. After that Killbee began to see a champion in Jim Greer, who lived with the Cronins.

He'd begun to get wind of something

that everybody in Killbee except himself appeared to know about. He had been living with the Cronins about a month before the old woman told him:

'Even though they'd been married only a few months, I could see Jim Brennan was getting tired of Mabel. He was growing too big for his shoes. Those were the days when logging was a gold-mine, and he was getting rich fast. And it wasn't hard to guess he ran around with other women when he went to Portland on business.

'Her dad and me had pleaded with her not to marry Jim Brennan, but she thought she knew all the answers, and Jim was used to getting everything he went after. He tried to keep her at the camp all the time at first, didn't want her to come home to see us. But afterward he didn't seem to care. He was getting ready to throw her over.

'She still loved him in a way, and she was quite dazed about it. She'd never known anything but love all her life, and now the only thing she had to love was her big bulldog, Caesar. Jim had given him to her when he was a pup. He was almost grown now, and he loved her better than he did any other human. They were always together.

'So I was surprised when Jim Brennan asked Mabel to accompany him on that hunting trip up the mountain. Him and Bill Jim, the Indian. Bill Jim was a savage, and a bad man. Him and Jim Brennan used to get drunk together — going off quietly. And stories used to come back about them . . . Well, that's neither here nor there. But I begged Mabel not to go. Somehow I knew I'd never see her again.

'Her dad begged her too, but she was self-willed and obstinate. And then, Jim Brennan could be so winning, when he wanted to be. I believe the poor child really thought she'd won his love again.

'They started off together, Bill Jim carrying the tent, and the axe, and the bag of food, Jim Brennan with his rifle, and Mabel with his fishing-rod. They were going right up Mount Crow, where Jim said there were mountain sheep, but he'd never got one yet. It was my lamb who was to be the victim.'

Jim Greer realized now that this was what had made the Killbee folks look furtive whenever Mabel's name was mentioned in his presence. He'd known that she had fallen over a crevasse, and that her body hadn't been found — now he sensed something worse than tragedy: murder.

The old woman said:

'She turned and waved to me. That was the last I ever saw of her. And that was the last anybody ever saw of Bill Jim. Brennan came back alone.'

The sheriff waited till Mrs. Cronin could compose herself. Old Cronin came into the room and watched them, standing by the door, silent.

'It was two days later when Jim Brennan came back alone. There was a long gash across his forehead, and his hands were cut and bruised. He told how Mabel and Bill Jim had both fallen through the snow upside-down into a crevasse, which even the Indian hadn't known was there — fallen down a sheer two hundred feet into the snow that covers the Crow glacier. It had all happened in a moment — '

'And the dog jumped after them,' put in old Cronin.

'He'd tried to climb down the rocks, but there's no way down those rocks. We got a search-party together, and started up the shore of the Crow River, and along the glacier. I went with them, as far as I was able.

'I had to turn back. They did their best, but there was nothing to mark exactly where they had fallen. And the snow's fifty foot deep — maybe a hundred. Snowshoes ain't much use on that snow, which is full of sink-holes where a man might go clear down to the glacier underneath. And tons of avalanches falling from above, at that time of the year.

'And there wasn't the slightest hope. Nobody had had any hope from the first. But I knew — and everybody knew — that Jim Brennan had murdered his wife up there.'

'And the Indian?' queried the sheriff.

'Brennan murdered him too,' said old Cronin. 'He had to. Brennan wasn't the kind of man who would live all the rest of his life in fear of being blackmailed. He killed the two of them. But there's vengeance coming. The hand of the Lord is slow to work, but He never lets up on the guilty.'

His wife turned her eyes upon him, and Sheriff Greer thought he could detect a warning in that look. A warning not to say anything more. It seemed as if there still was something connected with the death of Mabel Brennan that he hadn't been told, though all the older inhabitants of Killbee knew about it.

He spoke out: 'You know, folks, it's the practice of Anglo-Saxon jurisprudence to consider every man innocent until he has been proved guilty. If there's any reason to believe Mr.

Brennan guilty, beyond surmise, tell me what it is and I'll look into it — I don't care how many years have passed.'

'Leave it to God, son,' answered Cronin. 'He'll see to it that His innocent ones, whose blood cries unto Him, are avenged.'

In early summer, Brennan arrived. Flaherty was waiting for him in Killbee when his car rolled in, and the two went off together to the camp. Not far from it was the hunting-camp that Brennan had built. Aggie Quinn, who had put the place in order, and had been awaiting Brennan's arrival, reported that the two men were on the best of terms — and drinking hard.

'They were talking about the sheriff,' she confided to her circle. 'Flaherty was saying he's too damn independent. Mr. Brennan was asking him a lot of questions about him. They'll sure make trouble for Mr. Greer.'

Jim Greer was expecting trouble when Brennan sent word that he'd like to see him. However, trouble was his business. He dropped in at the camp on the afternoon appointed, to find Brennan rather different from what he had thought he would be. He was a large, fleshy man, with prominent blue eyes, grizzling hair — in his early fifties, Jim would have said. His handclasp was friendly, and he didn't bring up the subject of the quarrel with Flaherty for some time.

Jim spent an agreeable two hours with him. Brennan spoke of his early days, his struggle to put the lumber industry on its feet in that part of the State. He asked Jim if he was interested in hunting, and offered to take him into the big-timber country that still remained to be logged, to get some bighorns.

Jim felt himself drawn to Brennan. He looked at the massive horns that adorned the walls of the camp, listened to Brennan's stories; even drank a glass of whiskey with him. Some of the tales were tall ones — but then Brennan didn't spare the liquor.

Brennan liked good guns, good rods. He opened the biggest clasp knife Jim had ever seen, an immense blade folding into a great pearl handle, manipulated by a spring.

'I stabbed him to death with this,' he said. He was speaking of a grizzly, but Jim guessed it had been a black. He agreed to accompany Brennan on one of his trips, if his time permitted. Actually he was becoming more and more interested in Mrs. Cronin's story.

Blustering, good natured, Brennan didn't seem to him the sort of man who would have been guilty of such an atrocious murder.

Just before Jim left, Brennan alluded to the trouble with Flaherty. 'I've told him he was off his beat,' he said. 'We're working with the law and the authorities. Don't worry about him; I'll stand by you.'

Jim hadn't any real intention of going on a trip with Brennan, but he rather liked the man. He liked Killbee, too. He came from a small town sixty miles away, where he had made something of a reputation by running down a murderer. Killbee, which had depended entirely on the lumber company, had become disgusted when some of Flaherty's crowd had trouble in town, on pay nights, instead of going to some of the recognized centers for their amusement.

There had been bad blood, and it hadn't been improved by the beating up of old Cronin. But, since Jim tangled with Flaherty, the lumber crowd had been lying low. And now, with Brennan's declaration, a period of profound peace descended on Killbee.

Jim got to love the people and the land. He liked to walk out along the mountain trail, to the point where the Crow glacier discharged its foaming torrent that supplied power to the logging mill. It was spring now, and almost each day one could trace the spread of the verdure higher and higher up the slope. Sometimes Jim would spend an afternoon tackling the trout that were swept down in the rush of water, struggling madly to swim back against the force of the stream. Sometimes he brought back a sizable catch for supper at the Cronins.

The boys were out, too, all along the bank of the river, some, bolder than the rest, clambering along the edge of the glacier, where it reared itself in a mighty wall above the torrent.

Jim had no rod the day he met old Cronin. He was strolling along the bank when he saw the old man, standing patiently, rod in hand, though he was half crippled with arthritis. 'Catch anything?' he called.

Cronin looked at him in a curious way. 'Not yet,' he said briefly. Somehow Jim was getting the idea that his presence was not altogether welcome to old Cronin. He was thinking of having a house built — there was a girl back in Drummond. He didn't quite know what he was waiting for. He had built his local reputation with his arrest of the lumberjack. He just felt that it

212

might be wiser to wait awhile. If you'd asked him why, he couldn't have answered.

Brennan hadn't done much hunting, but he'd done a good deal of drinking. Jim had been driving past the camp to investigate a petty quarrel at the logging mill — nothing of any consequence, as it turned out. Driving back, he saw Brennan sitting on the porch of his camp, and stopped at his hall.

'How are you, Greer?' Brennan called. 'I hear there was some trouble up at the mill. Mind coming in and telling me about it?'

Jim got out and went inside with Brennan, who was quite drunk, following him. He accepted the glass of whiskey Brennan offered him.

Brennan, sprawled in a chair, said, 'I'm leaving day after tomorrow, Greer, and between you and me, I doubt whether I'll ever return to this place. I've had a good offer, and I'm thinking of selling out. It gets under my skin, coming back year after year to the place

I grew up in as a boy, where there used to be friendly folks.'

'That'll be too bad,' said Jim. 'We'll miss you, Mr. Brennan.' He almost felt it, too.

Brennan uttered a short laugh. 'I guess you haven't been here too short a time not to have heard about things that happened once,' he said.

'If I understand you — ' parried Jim.

'Oh, yeah, you understand me. I'm speaking about my wife. You haven't been staying with the Cronins without picking up something about it. It was twenty years ago, and it's all past history now, but it was a mighty tragic thing to me, Greer. You see, I loved her.'

There was a sincerity in Brennan's words that found a response in Jim's heart. He wasn't often mistaken in his judgment of men. He'd always claimed that a lawman should have a fifth sense that enabled him to form his judgment, even in despite of the evidence. And he liked Brennan, though he was sitting there before him three-parts drunk and reaching the maudlin state.

Coarse, blustering, overbearing, he had nevertheless a fundamental sincerity about him. He reached out for the bottle, offered a drink to Greer, who shook his head, and refilled his own glass.

'I've never told anyone the whole truth yet,' he said. 'Now that I'm quitting Killbee for good —

'We'd camped in a stretch of woods beside the gorge, my wife, Bill Jim, our Indian guide, and me. It was too rough-going for a girl, but Mabel had pleaded to come with me, and I'd agreed. It wasn't too cold, and we had plenty of blankets, and Bill Jim lit a roaring fire.

'He'd been drinking, and I'd been drinking more than I'd ought. That Indian devil was a queer fellow, sullen and suspicious, and he could put away enough liquor to send you or me under the table, and yet I'd never seen him change or show it. He'd guided me for years, and I thought I could trust him anywhere.

'Mabel and me had had a tiff that morning, I'll admit, over some damned stupid thing — sort of thing most young married people fall out over. And her mother hated me — I never found out why. She was always telling my wife I was no good. I'd had some sort of hope when I got her away alone we could talk things over, and patch up our differences. I guess she thought so too. That was why I let her come with me.

'I'd started on ahead, and Mabel said she'd walk with the guide. I was proud and stubborn, and let her have her way. I must have been three hundred yards ahead when I heard her scream. I turned, and saw her and Bill Jim struggling together on the edge of the glacier. The dog was barking furiously.

'I understood what was happening. I'd always trusted that Indian, but the liquor must have made a madman out of him. I tried to shoot him, but it was impossible to aim and fire from that distance without the chance of killing Mabel.

'I ran back, shouting. He paid no attention. And before I was halfway there, the two disappeared together over the edge into the snow-covered glacier. The dog, too. I was left alone.

'I tried to climb down, but had to give up the idea as hopeless. I pulled myself together. I hurried back. But I didn't say about the Indian going crazy. I guess I was afraid, Greer, afraid of taking the blame for leaving my wife with him. That's all. Thank God I've been able to tell the truth at last.'

Brennan burst into sobs. Jim never quite remembered how he got out of the camp. He was thankful he had managed to pull himself together by the time he reached the Cronins.

Which version was true? Did Brennan suspect that all Killbee looked upon him as the murderer of his wife? Jim wasn't easily taken in by murderers' explanations, and Brennan had had twenty years to think up his — if the story was a lie.

It was possible, of course, that Brennan hadn't told him the whole truth. Brennan might actually have shot the Indian and concealed the fact. But that would have been morally and legally justified. All in all, Jim was convinced that Brennan's story was in the main true, even though he might not have been as much in love with his wife as he imagined, looking back over the years.

Jim had set up his office in the house occupied by the post-office. He hadn't much — a borrowed table and two chairs, a few law books, a few notices from the Federal Government and neighboring sheriffs, tacked up on the walls. He was making his way toward it the following morning when he heard a commotion up the river.

Boys were shouting, and people were streaming up toward the glacier from the village. Among them he saw the Cronins, the old woman helping her crippled husband, who was hobbling with his stick.

A man came running toward Jim from the direction of his office. 'Sheriff, you're wanted over there — quick!' he shouted.

Jim wondered how the man knew; he hadn't come from the direction of the gesticulating crowd. Nevertheless, without stopping to ask any questions, he hurried toward it. The crowd was huddled together, staring down at the river, on the bank of which a boy was struggling with a fishing-line. They opened to make way for Jim, looking at him in silence. Jim went to the bank.

The river was racing from beneath the wall of ice, which towered up, steel-blue, translucent in the light of the morning sun. Whatever the boy was tugging at seemed firmly anchored under that wall; in the very heart of the torrent of racing water. It couldn't be anything but a monster trout that had taken refuge under the ice.

Then Jim saw. It was the white hand

and arm of a woman, protruding out of those depths, and the hook was taught higher up, in the shoulder or body that was still kept back by the ice-pressure.

And then he understood, and a shudder of horror ran through him. The glacier was giving up its long-since dead. And the Cronins had known — all Killbee had known the exact annual progress of the glacier down the bed of the stream. They had measured it exactly, and had awaited the murderer's victim to return that spring. That was why the boys had gone fishing there.

Old Cronin caught Jim by the arm. He pointed, jabbering to that arm. 'I said that the Lord would avenge His own,' he cried triumphantly.

A sudden jerk of the line, and the body came into view. A universal groan went up as it suddenly came free. In an instant it was caught up by the stream, and bobbed grotesquely on the hook as the race of water sought to tear it free and send it hurtling downstream. One of the men snatched the pole from the boy's hands, and maneuvered the body against a mass of dead branches caught in an angle of the bank. A dozen men dipped into the shallows, and bore it ashore.

It was the body of a young and beautiful girl, perfectly preserved by the ice that had held it intact for twenty years. The clothing, however, had dissolved almost to the consistency of a thick paste, which coated the body, like a tight-fitting undergarment.

Cries of horror and rage broke out. So perfectly had the glacier retained the secret that it was possible to see the black streaks upon the face that showed where the girl had been bruised. And, wedged firmly between the ribs, was the handle of a knife, whose blade must long since have rusted away. It must have penetrated the heart, producing instant death.

It was a very large pearl-handled implement that looked as if it must have formed part of a clasp-knife. Jim looked hard at it, wondering where he had seen a knife like that before.

Then suddenly he knew. So did they all. Old Mrs. Cronin had fallen on her knees in prayer beside the body; her husband stood beside her, muttering and half-dazed. But the crowd was dissolving, racing back toward the trail that ran to Brennan's camp.

Jim's place was with the body. He remained there, while the two old people, as if unconscious of his presence, mumbled and prayed. The shouting had died away in the distance, but now it was audible again. Perhaps half-an-hour had passed before the mob rounded the curve of the trail and came toward the body.

With them was Brennan, but Brennan walking erect and defiant, and commanding fear from the crowd that yelled and surged about him, yet dared not lay a hand upon him.

Nevertheless, Brennan faltered when he saw the body on the ground. For a moment he seemed to sway, and clapped his hand to his forehead. At that sign of weakness the mob closed in. Jim Greer intervened.

'Out of the way, everyone,' he ordered. 'Mr. Brennan, I've got to take you in on the charge of murder.'

Jim rushed his prisoner to the county seat at Drummond, his home town, and got him ensconced in the strong jail there. He reached Drummond just twenty minutes ahead of a mob of howling lumberjacks, intent on rescuing their chief. In that twenty minutes he had time to swear in a dozen deputies, to prevent the freeing of the prisoner.

He was glad that the trial would take place with a minimum of delay. The situation was tense, with the lumberjacks sworn to free Brennan, and the whole county equally resolved to send Brennan to his death. There was time for a visit with a certain young lady, and then, his duties ended, Jim went back to Killbee.

He went through more than one change of mind during the interval before the trial. The Cronins positively identified the knife found in the body as one that Brennan had always carried. Those big clasp-knives with pearl handles had been a hobby of his. The Cronins were exultant. Jim, in the face of the universal exultation, remained non-committal. As he said, his only job now was to marshal the witnesses and attend the trial.

'You sure seem to be taking it easy, Sheriff,' drawled one of the Killbee men, as Jim passed up the trail, carrying his fishing-pole. 'But I guess you feel you've earned a vacation, pulling in that damned killer.'

Jim shrugged his shoulders. 'We've got to convict him before we can call him that,' he answered.

The other stared. 'You mean you don't think him guilty?' he demanded.

'Twenty years is a long time,' said Jim.

'Yeah, but that knife — why, everybody knows Brennan has always used knives like that.'

'Maybe the Indian stole it from him.'

The other cackled. 'That line won't go down with a jury from this county. They won't want too much evidence to convict a skunk like Brennan.'

Jim passed on and did some fishing, turning things over in his mind. He was coming to believe more and more in Brennan's innocence. And he was pretty sure he was going to be convicted.

The Cronins received him and his string of trout coldly. Jim's observations two or three hours earlier had already been transmitted throughout the village. Folks were saying that Jim was queer.

The judge had denied an application for a change of venue. He was convinced that justice could well and truly and diligently be administered by the good citizens of the county. Jim got a permit to see Brennan a day or two before the trial opened. He found him confident, but bitter. Brennan's lawyer had advised him that there was no case against him.

'I've supported Killbee long enough,' he raged. 'I told you I was getting out, didn't I? Well, I'm staying long enough to get contract labor up from the Coast, and I'll let Killbee whistle for its living.'

'Trouble is,' said Jim slowly, 'the county is kind of prejudiced, Mr. Brennan. You antagonized the labor element. And that's the element that's going to make up the jury.'

Brennan stared at him, then got the point. His lawyer, Simpson, was from California, an able man, but ignorant of conditions in Killbee and Drummond.

'So you think they'll convict me?' he demanded.

'I'm only saying you won't get a walk over,' answered Jim.

Brennan snarled: 'Maybe you too believe I'm guilty of this murder?'

'Well, now, it's not for a sheriff to express his opinions as to guilt or innocence,' Jim countered. 'However, I don't mind telling you I'm on your side. There's something like a fifth sense that every lawman ought to have, and it tells me you're innocent.'

'Thanks,' answered Brennan dryly.

'But you see,' said Jim, 'apart from the knife, you've told two conflicting stories. First time, you didn't say anything about that Indian being crazy drunk — just made out that him and your wife stepped into a crevasse. Second time, talking to me, you admitted seeing him attack your wife, but you'd been afraid to acknowledge it, for fear of being blamed for leaving them together. Maybe there's a third version coming, namely, that you shot the Indian dead, and maybe killed your wife by mistake.

'What you tell me ain't evidence, Mr. Brennan, but I might have a better chance of helping you if I knew which version is the correct one.'

'The one I told you,' said Brennan. 'I didn't shoot Bill Jim. I couldn't, for fear of hitting my wife.'

'You'll stick to that in court?'

'I certainly shall.'

'They'll bring up what you said twenty years ago. Mind if I see your lawyer?'

'Not in the least,' said Brennan.

Folks wondered why the sheriff was so busy in those days. He was scurrying back and forth between Killbee and Drummond daily, now measuring and examining the terrain along the glacier trail, now conferring with officials in Drummond.

His court duties were nominal, there being another sheriff in the county town who was charged with the local duties. But he interviewed both the prosecuting attorney and Brennan's lawyer, Simpson. The prosecutor was an earnest young man, determined to make a name for himself by obtaining a verdict of guilty against the big man of the district, whose sensational arrest had brought a crowd of newspapermen and photographers to the little county town.

'We've got a representative jury,' he chuckled, 'and there won't be a lumberman on it. Brennan hasn't a dog's chance, the way feeling is running against him.'

'You're convinced he's guilty?' asked Sheriff Jim.

'Guilty? Of course he's guilty. He'd wanted to get rid of his wife. The Cronins will prove that. He went off hunting with her. His knife was found in her body. And then presumably he shot and killed the Indian, to keep his mouth closed. Any jury would convict on that chain of evidence.'

As for the defendant's lawyer, Simpson, he had by now realized the situation his client was in. Brennan must have told him that the sheriff was on his side, for he received Jim warmly. He appeared to be a man in a state of bewilderment,

'There's a feeling I don't like,' he admitted. 'What evidence is there against Brennan? Nothing but that knife. Brennan admits it's his. But that Indian might readily have picked it up and used it to kill the wife with. You couldn't convict a man on that sort of evidence anywhere but in these parts.'

Jim said slowly: 'Looks like we'll have to hope for a miracle, Mr. Simpson.'

'You're convinced that he's innocent?'

'I am,' said Jim. 'Look, Mr. Simpson, I'm not going to be at the trial. But I'm going to have a line put through from my shack at Killbee to the courthouse. If anything turns up, I'll call you.'

'What could turn up?'

'I'm making investigations — ain't finished yet,' said Jim. 'There's one good thing about miracles: they turn up just when they're most needed.'

Judge Barton had been the head of the law school from which Jim graduated. Whether or not the sheriff had approached him on the subject of Brennan's guilt or innocence, it was obvious that he disapproved of the way the trial was going.

Simpson's peremptory challenges had failed to obtain a jury that was free from the bitter prejudice manifest in the courtroom. First the Cronins, and then witness after witness came forward to testify as to the defendant's brutality toward his wife. This established, Mrs. Cronin became the star witness regarding Brennan's ill-fated hunting trip with his wife and the Indian, and his return alone.

'You recognize this knife-handle, Mrs. Cronin?' inquired the prosecutor blandly.

'I surely do. James Brennan always carried that knife, or one like it. Maybe he had one like it made after he'd buried the first one in my daughter's body.'

The judge's gavel hammered several times, 'You are here to give evidence, not to make inferences,' said Barton. 'The jury will disregard the suggestion.'

But the mischief had been done. And Brennan didn't help his case when he took the stand to give his evidence as to what had occurred along the trail.

The honest but obtuse doggedness of the man was lost on all except Judge

Barton. The prosecutor was on his feet the moment Brennan had ended.

'You say that this Indian attacked your wife, that you were afraid to fire for fear of hitting her, and that the two disappeared over the edge of the glacier before you could reach her?' he asked suavely.

'That was my evidence.'

'The story you told twenty years ago contained no reference to such an attack. Why was that?'

Brennan said doggedly: 'I was afraid I'd be blamed for having left my wife to follow with Bill Jim.'

'You were a coward?'

'Call it that, if you want to.'

'Do you expect the jury to believe such a preposterous story as you are now telling them?'

'I don't care if they believe it or not,' shouted Brennan, reverting to his old bluster. 'It's true!'

'Please take your witness,' said the prosecutor to Simpson.

The trial ended on the day that it

began, and the verdict was a foregone conclusion. When Judge Barton pointed out to the jury the necessity of dismissing all prejudice from their minds, they stirred uneasily in their seats, but it was plain their minds were already made up. The prosecutor had excelled all former efforts in the excoriating speech he made in surre-buttal. It was beginning to grow dark when the judge dismissed them, with the notification that he would receive their verdict at any time prior to midnight.

The spectators remained in their seats, anticipating a speedy verdict. What delayed this was the inevitable non-conformist, who held out stoutly for an acquittal on the ground that the evidence was insufficient to convict. It was past eleven o'clock at night before he yielded to the indignant clamor of the weary eleven.

The judge, summoned from his room, came into the courtroom. Brennan was brought up from his cell. He faced the twelve, a sneer upon his face. The clerk said: 'Gentlemen of the jury, are you agreed upon your verdict?'

'We are,' said the foreman.

'How say you, do you find the defendant, James Brennan, guilty or not?'

A figure dashed into the court. 'Hold everything!' it yelled. Simpson was standing breathless between the jury and the clerk of the court.

'Your honor, evidence — new evidence — turned up — ' he gasped. 'I'm asking — court be adjourned to Killbee — to present new evidence — '

The prosecutor was on his feet, with a roar of protest. 'This is quite irregular, your honor,' he shouted. 'There is no precedent for such a motion — '

The gavel fell. 'Your motion is that this court be adjourned to Killbee?'

'Till 'tomorrow morning,' gasped Simpson, still out of breath. 'Transportation furnished — complete refutation of this charge.'

'I protest!' shouted the prosecutor.

'If you have new evidence to present in behalf of your client,' said Judge Barton, 'I am prepared to adjourn this court until tomorrow morning when it will resume here — '

'Sheriff Greer has just phoned me from Killbee that he has arrested the murderer of Mrs. Brennan, and is holding him there,' said Simpson. 'He asks that the court adjourn there, to save the county the expense of a protracted trial.'

That was one in the eye for the prosecutor, whose repeated objection was drowned in the general upheaval. Judge Barton said: 'This court will reassemble at Killbee at nine o'clock tomorrow morning.'

It was six o'clock, and growing light, when the grumbling jurors, more firmly resolved than ever — except for their one non-conforming member — to find the defendant guilty, started on the ride along the bumpy road. A string of cars filed out of Drummond, Judge Barton in the lead, with the court clerk, then the prosecutor, driving his own, then the jury in three, then Simpson.

Trailing behind came a dozen cars filled with inhabitants of Drummond, prepared to see the matter through.

The excitement in Drummond was as nothing in comparison with that in Killbee, where the populace was drawn up en masse, with Sheriff Greer at their head; to greet the newcomers. As the leading car came to a halt, the judge asked: 'Well, Jim, where's the court-room?'

Jim grinned, and pointed along the river trail. Slowly it began to dawn upon the jury that they were expected to hold court under the sky, after a walk of more than a mile along a trail.

But, as they walked, the rumor of what had happened began to permeate them. The body of the Indian — released from the glacier by the sheriff's hooks and lines — hedged in with ice-blocks . . .

The foreman said: 'I dunno what's

the matter with the judge, but this don't faze me none. Guilty as hell, boys, whether that Indian's body has been found or not. What do you say?'

Ten voices assented, and the eleventh was hushed. They'd bring him around. Nobody's temper had been improved by the night waiting, the bumpy ride, the tramp along the spring-sodden banks under a drizzling rain.

When they stopped beside the roaring stream, and the towering mass of the glacier's edge, they could see nothing at first, on account of the crowd. It took considerable effort on the sheriff's part to get the jury to the edge of the river, where lay the body of Bill Jim, perfectly preserved after his icy habitation of twenty years.

He lay there, curled up on his side, the scowl of insane rage still stamped on one side of his face. Against the other side, its teeth fixed firmly in the throat, was the body of the dead woman's bulldog.

As they took in the implication, a

dead silence fell. Sheriff Jim said softly: 'It sort of shows who was the killer of Mabel Brennan, don't it, gentlemen?'

We do hope that you have enjoyed reading this large print book.

Did you know that all of our titles are available for purchase?

We publish a wide range of high quality large print books including:
Romances, Mysteries, Classics
General Fiction
Non Fiction and Westerns

Special interest titles available in large print are:
The Little Oxford Dictionary
Music Book, Song Book
Hymn Book, Service Book

Also available from us courtesy of Oxford University Press:
Young Readers' Dictionary
(large print edition)
Young Readers' Thesaurus
(large print edition)

For further information or a free brochure, please contact us at:
Ulverscroft Large Print Books Ltd.,
The Green, Bradgate Road, Anstey,
Leicester, LE7 7FU, England.
Tel: (00 44) **0116 236 4325**
Fax: (00 44) **0116 234 0205**

NOTHING MORE TO LOSE

Tyler Hatch

The day Buck Buckley foils the Green River bank robbery is the day he becomes a hero with a capital 'H' — although the attention that follows is the last thing he wants or needs. Locals can't understand Buckley's resistance, but they do not know the secrets he is hiding. When his picture appears in the papers, his past begins to catch up with him. And as his newfound fame puts him in the firing line, he must stop running and address his demons face on in a final showdown.

VALLEY OF THUNDER

Sam Clancy

Josh Ford is the best man the Marshal Service has ever had, so when the governor of Montana needs someone to look into the disappearance of wagon trains in the Bitterroots, Ford is the man he chooses. What Ford finds is a brutal autocrat who rules with terror unlike Ford has ever seen. Across the northwest, he must fight against a maniac and his small army — but when a final twist puts it all in jeopardy, he realizes that the badge he wears may be the difference between law and justice.

RELUCTANT TIN STAR

Dale Graham

When Marshal Troy Garrison is forced to leave the Colorado town of Aguilar under a cloud, he figures he's done with the law for good. Heading south into New Mexico, he becomes embroiled in a series of unsavoury incidents culminating in his rescue of a damsel in distress. An unscrupulous gang of rustlers is terrorizing the area, and Troy reluctantly pins on the tin star once again. But when the woman's brother becomes involved with the gang, he is forced to choose between romance and upholding the law . . .